Silver Skin

Joan Lennon has had lovely stories and poems published for readers of all ages, all over the world. She appears regularly at book festivals, libraries and schools throughout the UK, giving talks and leading workshops for readers and writers.

SILVER
SKIN

JOAN LENNON

Dedicated to Lindsey Fraser,
the best agent/editor/champion
a book or writer could ask for

First published in 2015 by
Birlinn Limited
West Newington House
10 Newington Road
Edinburgh
EH9 1QS

www.birlinn.co.uk

ISBN: 978 1 78027 284 9

British Library Cataloguing-in-Publication Data
A catalogue record for this book is available from the British Library

Typeset by Iolaire Typesetting, Newtonmore
Printed and bound by Grafica Veneta
www.graficaveneta.com

PART ONE

Mrs Trevelyan: Mid Victorian Age, by the Bay of Skaill, Orkney

She woke in the winter dark, still half in the dream. She clutched the covers and felt her heart thudding against her ribs as the wind shrieked and moaned round the house. *Lost souls ... why does it sound like lost souls?* The window frames rattled as if shaken by desperate hands, trying to get in. Sand from the shore hissed against the glass. *Who are you?* She sat up. *I can't help you – I can't! I can't!* But the dream voices went on crying and wailing.

Sudden lightning slashed the blackness, thunder right on its heels before she could even begin to count.

The storm must be directly overhead. That's what woke me, she told herself firmly.

She lit a candle – there wasn't gas laid on, with the house being so remote. The flame flickered and bent in the draft from the windows.

It was a far cry from Edinburgh – *which is exactly what I wanted,* she reminded herself.

She thought of the day Mr Trevelyan first brought her to the island they called the Mainland, to see what would be her new home. He'd planned for her to have one of the big main bedrooms at the front of the house for her own – had even offered what had once been his mother's, God rest her – but she'd asked instead for the room that looked back towards the sea and the green hump so quaintly named the Howe of the Trows, out to the grey headlands and the long white beach. When it was calm, she'd explained, she loved the soft sounds of the waves on the sand.

'Well, and when there's a storm, what then?' he'd said and straight back she'd answered,

'Better to look your enemy in the eye than to turn your back.'

She'd heard her father say things like that her whole life, and the words just popped out.

'Or so my father says,' she'd added quickly. Humbly.

She knew what Mr Trevelyan was thinking. *Now she's about to be a married woman, shouldn't it be MY sayings that she hears in her head? I never say things like that. Too fanciful. I'd have thought better of the old man.*

He was remarkably transparent.

'I love this house,' she murmured, watching him from under her eyelashes. 'And I do love this room.'

And he'd given it to her, just like that, all magnanimous. He'd even patted her arm. It was an odd sensation, but she found she didn't mind. Her father had chosen a decent man for her, even if there was a gap between their ages. Her mother had taken her aside on the wedding morning and given her some quiet information and advice – some of it quite surprising, though now she knew it to be almost entirely true.

The proposal and the preparations, the marriage ceremony itself – it had all passed by so quickly. Almost like a dream. And then her father kissed her on the forehead as he handed her into the carriage, and murmured, 'God bless you, Mrs Trevelyan.' That had been the moment she'd realised it was all . . . real.

She was a woman now. Twenty next birthday, lately

4

returned from her wedding trip on the Continent, with a husband and a fine house to run, on a fine island estate – a bit wild, a bit remote, it was true, but substantial. Something to be proud of. Something to build a life out of.

The house shook.

We never had storms like this in Edinburgh, she thought. *Nothing exciting ever happened there.*

She slipped out of bed and drew back the curtains at the window. There was nothing but blackness to see. Blackness, and the white smudge of her face reflected in the glass.

She shivered and retreated to her bed again. The draft from the window rustled the pages of the book she'd been reading. Not exactly in secret, but there was no point in waving it about in Mr Trevelyan's face. *Dante's Inferno.* She'd bought it on a whim, when Mr Trevelyan wasn't looking, in an English book shop in Rome. She knew what he'd say – *Fancies. And foreign fancies at that!* – but she was enchanted and moved by the story. It was so sad, so achingly sad, especially the way the poet wrote about the Second Circle of Hell, the one where lovers were punished, swept about forever in an endless wind, so that they could never find rest. It was clear Dante had suffered from the pain of love, the grand passion she'd read about, in other books Mr Trevelyan would not have approved of.

She gave herself a mental shake. No wonder she was having bad dreams, and hearing voices in the storm. Fancies. That was all it was. Nothing more.

The storm shrieked and moaned and beat about the walls. Mrs Trevelyan wrapped a soft shawl of fine wool tightly around her shoulders. She watched the little flame thrashing on the candle wick and waited for the morning.

Rab: Age of the Alexander Decision, Tower Stack 367–74/ Level 56, Delta Grid, Northwest Europasia

'Oh, come on – not a storm as well!' moaned Rab, but his friends just laughed.

'You can do it, Rab!'

'Bet you're wishing you still had that knife, eh?'

Chillingly realistic rain was now drenching all the participants, but none of the others were having to wrestle with a wolf at the same time.

'Com? Com! I could do with some help here!' said Rab, desperately trying to keep the wolf from closing its jaws on him. It was growling continuously and its breath stank disconcertingly of half-digested meat.

'As your friend suggests, your options at this point are substantially fewer since you broke the knife at the last level,' said his Com. It was sounding smug, since it had advised strongly against using a knife on a rhinophant. It was also safe from the wind and the rain, lodged in Rab's wrist unit.

'Yeah, yeah. Get on with it.'

'So at this point you could either a) strangle the beast, which, given the average historical thickness of wolf neck fur and the digital reach and compressible strength of your hands, has only a zero point six per cent chance of success, or b) engage Vulcanski's Pack-Mind Manipulation Gaze. Since the Gaze is almost certainly fictional I have no statistics on the likelihood of its success, but it would certainly have the element of surprise.'

'That's all you've got?'

'Yes.'

Rab groaned as the wolf arched suddenly and almost wrenched itself free.

'Or . . .' said his Com.

'OR WHAT?!'

'Or you could just let go and see what happens.'

Thanks, thought Rab. He tried to remember what he knew about the Vulcanski Gaze. *I think there's no blinking.* He shifted himself round until he could see the wolf's eyes. The close quarters made it go squinty. *And then I pour all my innate superiority into its skull – no doubts, no uncertainty – I'm the Alpha male – that's me, not you – you are inferior – you are inferior – you are . . .*

The wolf burped, but showed no other sign of being intimidated.

'Hey, Rab! Your mum's here,' one of his friends called.

Rab risked a glance over to the observation booth. His mum was waving something – a package – at him. But while the simulation programme was running, she couldn't come in.

'Work with me here,' Rab whispered so only the wolf could hear. 'My mum's watching . . .'

There was a brief pause while the wolf thought about this. Rab had the distinct impression it was reliving moments of its own cubhood. A look passed between them, and Rab carefully loosened his grip . . .

In elaborate slow motion, the wolf lowered its head, tucked its tail between its legs, flattened its ears. Rab maintained his gaze. The wolf began to back away . . .

'Look at that!' said his Com. 'It's working!'

And the wolf disappeared.

Rab leapt into the air. 'Yay! Ha! Me – ONE. Canis lupus – NIL. Rab is OFF the menu!' And he pranced across the floor, doing a wild gangly victory dance. The others joined in, three young men who had momentarily forgotten their dignity.

From the observation room, Rab's mum smiled at her tall brown son. He'd been working so hard, for so long – she couldn't remember the last time he'd just taken the time out to be silly. His friends too, of course. They'd all been studying and researching and writing and analysing – whatever their chosen subjects, they were all desperate to acquire enough credits to move out of their parents' spaces. Ever square centimetre of living space in every tower stack in the world had to be earned.

She glanced down at the package she was carrying.

Rab deserved the best chance, the best equipment his mother could provide. And the *Retro-Dimensional Time Wender with Full Cloaking Capability* – the one they called the Silver Skin – was it. It was the future of historical research. It was what her Rab needed to move ahead. To move out.

She tried to imagine what it would be like to have her space to herself again, after all these years, but her mind shied away.

Her Com heard her sigh. 'I know,' it said. 'But it's time.'

And then Rab came in, freshly sanitized and glowing with excitement.

'It's *come?*' he yipped.

'It's come?' echoed his Com, going squeaky.

'It's come.' And she handed Rab the package.

He stared at it, his brown eyes wide. The reports

– *first-hand* reports, not just something from sources – he could produce with a cutting edge tool like the Silver Skin – it would be amazing . . . His studies in history so far had got him on the way to a tiny unit of his own, but with this, who knows – he might even manage a window!

'Mum – *thank* you!' And he enveloped her in a rare, rough hug. A tiny part of his mind wondered, *When did she get so small?* But the rest was too excited to do anything but repeat over and over, *My own place! I'm going to earn my own place!*

Rab's Com had downloaded the extended manual and kept trying to read it aloud to him. 'The suit will protect us from danger – weapons discharged, for example, even at close quarters, will not be able to penetrate our molecular structure because of the sideways displacement – projectiles will simply pass through the space we'll be occupying, or *not* occupying – would you like me to read you the bit with the quantum physics?'

Rab raised a hand. 'No, no. That's fine.'

His Com sighed.

Rab sighed too. He was passionate about history and ecstatic about his new bit of kit, but he couldn't care less about its innards. He knew enough about the new time travel to know that it was ridiculously technical, but the basic premise boiled down to this: a traveller's position remained constant and time passed by them, rather than the other way around. So instead of Rab moving back and forth in time, time moved back and forth around Rab. Which was all fine and good, but so far he was just moving *himself* back and forth, in the tiny bit of his mum's unit where he slept.

'Come ON!' he groaned. The Silver Skin was lying there on his bed, shimmering tantalizingly. His Com just clicked at him and went on with its calculations. So Rab went back to pacing – three up, three back, three up, three back.

Ever since they'd first heard rumours about the Silver Skin – first started fantasizing about getting hold of one – Rab and his Com and his friends and *their* Coms had been arguing about which period of history it could be best used on.

The others all liked the Catastrophe Ages best, when things fell apart and the world teetered on the brink of annihilation – and Rab was tempted too. The Nadir, the Flood, the time referred to as The Bulge, just before the Alexander Decision finally managed to put a cap on the world's runaway over-population – near-disasters were always exciting, especially now that everything was so safe.

But the time for idle speculating was over. It was time to make a choice.

'If we want this to get noticed, we'd need something that hasn't already been done to death.'

'Pre-Nadir, then, do you think? But that still leaves an awful lot of history.'

'Something that's far enough back in time that there isn't a lot of vid evidence already available. Something like . . . Com! I did that project – remember? – on the First Industrial Revolution? That was Victorian – and they didn't even *have* vids. Or wait, no, they were just inventing cameras and stuff, but they were rubbish. No sound, no temperature control, no colour, single point of view – nothing.'

They discussed it back and forth, getting more and more excited. There were so many aspects of the time period that would be utterly fascinating to study at first hand. How could they possibly choose just one?

It was his Com who came up with the idea of Victorian archaeology.

'It was pretty much the beginning of that, wasn't it? Properly, I mean, not just bashing in, looting the gold, making wild guesses?'

Rab was delighted. 'That's *it* – but we won't do the sites everybody's heard about already. Not Egypt or China or Atlantis. Someplace obscure . . .'

And then it hit them.

'Someplace like right here?'

It was a brilliant idea. Every bit of the world had history of some sort – and the location of Tower Stack 367-74 was no exception. Fifty-six floors down was the site of the Orcadian Islands from long, long ago.

'Right under our feet!' His Com began to download co-ordinates into the Silver Skin's arm panel. 'Time: 1850, the year of the discovery of a Stone Age village which became known as Skara Brae. Place: what was then called Orkney and is now called – *here*! Stack 367-74, Delta Grid, Northwest Europasia. We'll use the big storm that winter – the one that blew away the sand, uncovering the village for the first time in thousands of years – as the anchor point. Neap tide. Full moon. Factor in a test stop . . . mid Deluvian . . .'

Rab wasn't really listening to the details. 'This is going to be amazing – they didn't have Coms or scanners or infra-beige – nothing! Just shovels and little brushes!'

'And now, it's time to download me!'

As the Com's download into the arm panel proceeded, the suit began to change. It shimmered more quickly, in and out of focus, like a heat wave or a mist. It was there, but only just.

Rab frowned. 'Are you sure it's my size? It's starting to look small.'

'What? Oh, don't worry. It will individualise to you when you put it on. It'll fit you like a second skin.'

Exactly like a second skin.

'I have to be naked?'

'Of course,' said his Com. 'The suit needs to make a perfect seal with your skin in order to function properly. It draws energy from your specific electrical field, for one thing, and for another, the cloaking mechanism is extremely finely tuned – even a millimetre out of alignment and it starts to fluctuate.'

'But . . .'

'Look at it this way – would you rather have a suit which makes you invisible, or one that leaves a pair of underpants walking about in history? I'm not at all sure Queen Victoria would approve.'

Rab was tempted. 'Is that *possible*?'

'No, of course not. Don't be silly. The suit just wouldn't work.'

'Spoilsport.'

He put it on. It was perfectly comfortable, and when he checked in the mirror, it covered him in mistiness up to the neck, while his head remained perfectly in focus.

'You won't be properly invisible until the helmet is on. That comes out of the suit when you press the button on the arm panel, there. The only tricky bit is making sure you keep your eyes open, otherwise you'll be stuck with them shut. Since anything touching your eyes makes them blink automatically, you'll need to apply a short-term response paralyser to your eyelids . . .'

'But won't my eyes dry out?'

'No,' said his Com. 'The suit provides lubrication as required. I can explain how, if you'd like . . .'

'No! No, that's all right,' said Rab, reaching for the paralyser and applying it to the outer corners of his eyelids.

'Excellent, excellent,' muttered his Com. 'Now press the helmet initiator on your arm panel . . . Here it comes!'

Rab felt something cool, almost like liquid, rising from the neck of the suit, up under his chin and onto his face, but as it covered his mouth and nose he couldn't help struggling for breath.

'Calm down – just breathe normally.' He could hear his Com's voice through the helmet's earpiece. 'The helmet draws oxygen from the surroundings, cleans it, and expels carbon dioxide as you breathe out. There, the seal's complete . . . It's not bad now, is it?'

And, really, it wasn't. Rab found that once he stopped *thinking* about breathing, he could do it just as if he weren't wearing anything over his face at all. He moved his arms experimentally and walked up and down a little.

'This is great!' He could speak without difficulty.

'Right. Now, you'll be able to move about without being detected, as long as you're careful not to knock into anything – or anyone. Remember, the Non-Intervention Contract's no joke. You can observe but you cannot interact. The clause on fines – well, put it this way, you'll be living in your mother's clothes closet from now to eternity and still be in debt. Oh, and remember you won't be able to eat or drink anything

13

while the suit's sealed, or, um, excrete anything either, but since the recommended first session is no more than two hours, that shouldn't be a problem.'

'I know, I know – are we ready?'

'There *are* more checks we really should do, this being our first go . . .' But the longing in his Com's voice was clear.

Rab grinned and with a big theatrical flourish, he brought his right arm up and over, finger heading for the control panel on his left forearm, and –

– a high-pitched whistling sounded in his ears – his vision blurred – he felt his stomach drop –

The blurring before his eyes cleared abruptly and Rab found he was squinting into bright sunlight – and the floor had disappeared! He was suspended high in the air over an enormous expanse of sparkling sea. He yelped and reached for something to catch hold of, but there was nothing there to grab.

His Com sighed in his earpiece. 'What did I say? Test stop, mid Deluvian, remember? Time moves around you, not the other way around, so if you start out 56 floors up in a tower stack and you go back to a time before the stack was built . . .?'

'Yeah, all right. I forgot. This is – this is *amazing* . . .'

The Deluvian Period had taken place during the height of the ocean rise, when the part of the Northwest Europasian continent that he lived in – *would* live in! – had been completely submerged.

'Look!'

Floating settlements undulated on the silvery winter swell below him like vast mats of seaweed, anchored to the mountains lying out of sight under the surface.

14

'Can't we go in closer?'

But his Com was already humming to itself in the way it did when it was happily engaged in calculations.

'Not today, not today. Here we go again . . . 19th century . . . 1850 . . .'

The blurring returned. Rab thought, *And next there'll be the I–just–lost–my–stomach thing and the whistling and then . . .*

He swore. 'SCUT! Com? *WHAT—?!*'

This was different – this was worse – much, *much* worse – the whistling was rising higher and higher, louder, a shriek that clawed at his ears – there was a blinding flash – a jolt that made his teeth rattle in his head – the shriek became a roar – Rab tried to shield himself but his arms wouldn't move. Just at the edge of hearing, he could make out his Com crying, '*This isn't right – this isn't supposed to—*' From nowhere something grabbed Rab in an enormous fist and squeezed, hard, so hard he felt his bones grind on one another and his eyes bulged and all the air rushed out of his lungs. His mouth opened and closed uselessly, like a stranded fish – darkness began to swallow him up – then, as if from far away, he heard his Com screaming into the black,

'WE'RE GOING DOWN – 19TH CENTURY – MAYDAY – MAYDAY—'

Cait: Late Stone Age, Bay of Skaill, Orkney

The sea fog was thick as wet wool. Cait turned back towards the village with a sigh. As she climbed the dune, the marram grass sliced at her legs and the gathering bag on her back leaked cold and wet.

She sniffed the damp air. The world was changing. It had rained all summer until the grain didn't even bother trying to grow or ripen, but just went straight to rotting in the field. And now the dark days had come again. It felt as if they'd only just left.

There was whispering in the village.

'Is it true?' little huddles of villagers murmured, looking over their shoulders. 'The times have never been so cruel – can you remember, ever? – not ever. They say the Sun is fading. Dying. What have we done? What can we do?'

The Old Woman heard the whispers too, but she just grinned her humourless grin and spent more time with the Old Chert's bones up at the cairn on the headland that overlooked the bay. She ate so little now she was starting to look like a corpse herself. Cait watched. She knew something was going on in the Old Woman's mind. She saw *something*. Oh yes, there was definitely something humping and twisting under the surface, but she didn't know what it was. And Voy – the Old Woman – wasn't talking. Well, not to her at least.

Cait flicked her wet hair away from her face. The world was changing all right. Except, it wasn't changing much for *her*. If she looked back or forward, all she could see was more of the same. Working for the Old Woman. Wanting to be away.

She pulled a face.

It felt so good, she pulled another – a horrible cross-eyed, mouth-twisting, tongue-poking face.

'This is what I think of *you*, Voy! And this! And THIS!' She dropped the bag and used both her hands to make the rudest gestures she knew. She pulled down her breeches and waggled her buttocks in the direction of the village, and when that got too cold she pulled them up again and did a wild *I hate you* dance up and down the dune for good measure.

As soon as she was back with the others, none of this must show in her face. But here, no one could see her. No one could hear her. It was as satisfying as scratching a midgie bite till it bled. She kept it up until she was out of breath.

Oh well.

She was just bending for the bag, ready to swing it onto her shoulder again . . .

. . . when she heard it.

A high-pitched whistling that made her instantly crouch, her legs tensed under her and her heart beating hard in her throat. *Where?* It sounded as if something were dropping out of the sky – *there!* Out in the bay. It hit the water hard. Cait strained her eyes but the fog was as impenetrable as ever.

She half-uncurled, poised to run, but there was silence now over the bay. The tide was coming in as a greasy swell in the still air. There wasn't a breath of wind to stir the white mist.

17

Sounds can travel strangely in fog. Maybe it was a sea bird, diving after fish. But she knew that wasn't right – no sea bird would be out fishing in weather like this. She shivered – but she didn't leave.

The fog condensed on her hair and trickled down her neck like cold fingers.

I'll wait till the tide's at the turn. It wouldn't be long now. And if nothing happened by then, she'd run every step of the way back to the village and say she'd heard killer whales spouting in the bay. With a fog this thick no one could prove she hadn't. *I heard them – a whole pod, it sounded like – spouting and splashing!* She rehearsed what she'd say in her head, getting the tone just right. Voy might beat her for not coming back to tell them sooner, but not as hard as she would if she thought Cait had just been shirking work. Or doing rude dances on the dunes . . .

She felt how her heartbeats had slowed again. Maybe it was stupid to stay even until the turn. Just asking for trouble. It wasn't as if the Old Woman needed an excuse to hit her. Especially since Gairstay, the Old Chert, died. She acted liked that was Cait's fault too but it wasn't. It wasn't! She'd done everything she could. She'd done everything Voy'd told her, everything she'd taught her, but the old man had just got iller and iller –

There!

Splashing.

Not killer whales, but splashing nonetheless. Something out in the bay, beating at the water, flailing, coming closer to shore. Her senses focused in on the sound. It felt wrong – it didn't belong. Animal? Bird? Fish? She listened – sniffed – she opened her mouth in case there was any

18

tang in the air she could taste – there *was* something . . .
it was odd . . . she didn't have any words for it . . .

Cait froze.

She could see it now, swirling the fog at the surface of
the swell, dragging itself through the shallows, out onto
the sand of the beach, and then . . .

. . . it pulled off its face.

Rab: Bay of Skaill

Rab was choking on panic, thrashing, desperately trying to clear away the horrible grey blurring of the air. He began to claw at the helmet, managing at last to drag it away from his face, but it made no difference. He was blind.

I can't see! I can't see! Why can't I see? Behind the beat of that fear, other questions clamoured for his attention. *Com? Where are you? Talk to me! Where am I? What's happened? Why can't I hear you . . .*

And then all the words in his head disappeared as his arm burst into flames.

Cait: Bay of Skaill

Even before the thing came blundering out of the sea and onto the sand, a word was forming in Cait's mind like a shiny pebble –

Selkie.

One of the Fey. The First People.

Everyone understood that humans shared the islands with kelpies, trows, banshees, ghouls. You knew where you were with humans but the Fey were tricksy and erratic, hard to predict and impossible to control.

And none more so than a selkie. A seal that could shed its silver skin and walk on land in human form. She knew from the stories how beautiful they were – how seductive – how whoever saw a selkie dancing on the shore was entranced, so that they couldn't bear the thought of it returning to its seal shape. They would steal its skin and hide it and for a time, everything would be well (better than well – ownership of a selkie's skin was a clear path to every luck and all prosperity) and the selkie would forget it had ever had any other form or home. Then, as sure as the sea beat on the shore, the wonderful new life would fall apart. The selkie would find its skin and vanish back into the waves, the days of good fortune and happiness disappearing with it.

Cait knew the stories – always starting with the luck, always ending with disaster. Anyone with any sense would think twice about walking into a story like that. Anyone with any sense would be running for the village this very minute and never look back.

Cait grimaced, made the sign against evil with her fingers, and crept closer along the ridge of the dune.

The selkie had collapsed on the sand. Even through the fog she could see the wetness gleaming on its strange, silvery skin. It was making ghastly, gasping noises. Then, impossibly, smoke began to rise from one of its limbs . . .

The scream it gave as it burst into flames made her heart flinch.

This can't be right! This can't be the way it happens!

The selkie was clawing at its silvery pelt, peeling it away, whimpering, frantic. It was skinning itself, like a rabbit carcass, right in front of her.

She wanted to help the creature – put it out of its agony – but she made herself pause for a heart beat.

Be smart for once in your life. Leave it – leave it –

Cait rose to her feet . . .

Rab: Skara Brae

Was he being carried? Why was he being carried? Such a long way – was it a long way? – the pain made him drop in and out of consciousness. Until, suddenly, he realised that the jolting had stopped. He was lying on his back in a dark, malodorous, smoky place.

Faces hung over him, drifting in and out of focus, grotesque faces that blurred and swirled and went away again.

'Who are you?' he whimpered. 'Why won't you help me?' The pain pulsed with each beat of his heart – a horrible, ugly, angry red – *how can it have a colour?* The smell of burnt flesh – *his* burnt flesh – made him retch but he had nothing left in his stomach – it felt as if it were his own insides he was trying to throw up.

'It hurts! It hurts!'

And then he remembered – he remembered *this*. Pain. He'd felt pain before. Once, when he was just a kid, he'd been showing off in an exercise class. He'd managed to fall awkwardly and broke his collar bone. His Com had him anaesthetised within the minute, and the bone was healed by the next day, but those seconds of agony had haunted him for weeks afterwards. Long, long seconds before the wonderful relief came – where was the relief? – and this pain was worse – much, much worse – and it was filling his whole body and the room and the world and it wasn't going away . . .

'Why doesn't it stop?'

And all they did was make the place he was in so hot he could hardly breathe and move him when he couldn't bear to be moved and gibber and speak nonsense he couldn't understand.

'Hot . . . too hot . . .'

Meanwhile the download shunt, placed under his scalp when Rab was a baby, was busy collecting language clues and ambient speech patterns, feeding them into its analytical database, collating, extrapolating, easing nouns and verbs and grammar and nuance into spare neural pathways. It was working furiously to give him a whole new language.

It was an exceptionally clever programme that the citizens of Rab's world had in their heads. The only question now was, would it have enough time to finish its task, or would the shock and growing infection and rising fever in Rab's body kill him first?

Cait: Skara Brae

The selkie groaned, thrashing restlessly in the bed box, disturbing the heather under the hide. Cait squatted on her heels, watching him, unconsciously rubbing the scratches on her legs.

She'd done everything she could think of. She'd bathed the burn with warmed sea water, applied crushed henbane leaves, dressed the selkie's arm with the fluff from the puffball fungus, given him bitter willow bark for the fever . . . Voy watched every move from the shadows, cradling her crippled hands, her eyes sharp – eager – for Cait to make a mistake. Now there was nothing left to be done. It was up to him, his strange body, and how strong his will was to survive.

She reached over to touch the pretty dark curls on his head, and felt the fever heat coming from him. If it didn't break soon, even will would have little to do with it.

Cait sighed.

She glanced over to the shelves where the spirit stones were kept and her thoughts fell into the old grooves. Four carved stones, where there should be five. One stone missing, all the years of her life . . .

If he does die, will Voy put HIS spirit in a stone and keep it to take with the others to the Ring? What were the rules that determined the fates of the Fey? Did Voy even know? *Perhaps they don't have spirits. Perhaps they ARE spirits.*

'Pay attention!' snapped Voy.

The selkie had thrown off the coverings again. He was muttering plaintively and though she couldn't catch the sense of his words, it was clear he was asking for something. Or someone. *It must be the seal language.* She'd heard their wailing before.

The feeling of guilt lodged in her throat, making it hard to swallow.

I should have left you by the sea, not told anyone about you. The other selkies might have come for you, if I hadn't interfered.

His own people would know how to make him better.

The burn on his arm continued angry and red. Streaks of inflammation ran up towards his shoulder and down into his hand. Familiar signs of infection, and yet . . .

It was the strangest wound she had ever seen.

Even Voy had been taken aback. She'd stared at the marks the fire had made on his skin for a long time, turning the selkie's arm roughly this way and that in the lamp light. He'd struggled weakly to get away from her, but she paid no attention, peering closely at the red inflamed pattern, as if she were trying to draw something important from it.

Healers dealt with burns all the time. There was an open hearth in every home. Babies learned the hard way that fire hurts; toddlers tumbled no matter how carefully their mothers watched them; cooking led to scalds; dried seaweed and dung fuel spat sparks unexpectedly. Everyone in the village carried scars.

But this burn was different. Instead of ugly, lumpy ridges on the flesh, his wound looked almost beautiful, as if it had been carved with the finest tool in the Stone

Maker's possession. Cait shook her head. No, not like that. Stone Makers created circles and swirls, but this was all thin straight lines and hard angles, intersecting squares and rectangles.

The nearest she'd ever seen to anything like this were the few scratched marks in the long passageway between the houses, that everyone touched for luck as they went by, even though no one knew what they meant any more or who had put them there. And there were the other ones, hacked into the edge of the Old Woman's bed and in the Chert's house. But they were clumsy things in comparison.

The pattern on his arm was strange. Like the selkie.

He didn't belong here.

Pity welled up in her throat.

She leaned close, taking the selkie's good hand in her own, trying to put comfort into the sound of her voice. 'Gently now, rest now. And as soon as you're well again, you can go back to the sea. Back to being a seal. Back to the cold and the waves . . .'

The sound of hissing laughter made the words die in her mouth. She bent her head and tilted it just enough to look across to the head of the hearth, through the smoke to where Voy squatted like a malignant toad.

The Old Woman was holding the selkie's skin, stroking it, running its silver sleekness through her twisted fingers. There was a look on her face that Cait couldn't read. But her eyes sparked and flickered strangely in the dim light, as if furious activity were going on behind them.

Never underestimate her, Cait. Never. . .

The selkie was shivering now. As she covered him with more fleeces, the thought came to her, *I'm sorry, seal boy* and then, *Maybe dying would be the kindest thing for you after all . . .*

'He can't die.'

Cait had fallen asleep leaning against the stone side of the bed, but Voy's voice jerked her awake. She rubbed her eyes, wondering how much time had passed. Voy was still crouched on her stone at the head of the hearth. Cait caught a glint of silver as the Old Woman finished stuffing the selkie's skin into a leather bag, tying it awkwardly to her belt.

'He can't die,' the Old Woman muttered again, staring into the embers. 'It is likely the power of the skin is tied to the human form. If that dies, it may be useless.'

Is she talking to me? thought Cait blearily.

Sometimes, lately, Cait would come in from gathering limpets or puffball fungus or the last of the shrivelled crowberries and Voy would be sitting, empty-faced, by the hearth. She'd let the fire go out, or the medicine she was distilling boil dry, and she'd be whispering to . . . no one. And even before, when the Old Woman spoke her thoughts aloud and it was just the two of them in the house, sometimes she would punish Cait for answering, and sometimes she would punish her for *not* answering. It was impossible to tell what to do, from one time to the next.

Cait stole a quick glance at the selkie. Still breathing, but his eyes were beginning to sink into his strange brown face as the fever ate at him from within. She had to speak. Speak for him. It was her fault he was here.

'If you don't want him to die, give him back his skin,' she said. Her voice sounded thin. She leaned forward and added fuel to the fire. 'Maybe his skin can heal him. He might be grateful and help us. If you keep it from him, and he dies, we might be haunted by his spirit. Who can say what damage that might do?' She held still, waiting to see if the Old Woman would respond.

Nothing. The smoke swirled up towards the roof, like a curtain of cloud between them. The selkie moaned softly. Cait took a breath.

'You *have* to give it back,' she persisted. 'You know the stories. You know no good comes of stealing a selkie's skin. Not in the end. It always goes wrong in the end.'

She saw Voy shift a little and show her teeth. They were still strong in spite of her age. 'That's because the people in the stories are always fools. I'm not a fool.'

'But—' Cait began again, when suddenly Voy lunged, grabbing her by the front of her tunic, dragging her forward till she was coughing in the smoke.

'Not all the people in the stories come to grief because of stupidity,' the Old Woman hissed. 'Sometimes it's because of greed – or betrayal. But I'm safe from all that. The people fear me. Even if they knew, they wouldn't tell the selkie where its skin is.'

And what about me? The words formed in Cait's mind against her will. This close, the Old Woman would surely read her thoughts in her eyes.

Voy did. '*You* would never betray me,' she whispered. 'You know what the price would be.' Then she let go, so suddenly Cait almost fell into the fire.

Oh, yes, thought Cait bitterly. *I know the price. I know it very well.*

Rab: Skara Brae

He woke and for a long moment he felt nothing but a deep woolly peace. His eyes drifted towards a shaft of sunlight that slanted down from the ceiling. It left everywhere else in darkness. *What a strange place . . .* It was like some sort of museum simulation. There was smoke drifting gently upwards. He stared at the slant of brightness. *Someone's made a hole in the ceiling. I wonder how they did that? Won't the people in the unit upstairs fall through?* He frowned. There was something he should be remembering. But it was hard to think – *like pushing a rock up a hill and it keeps slipping back again. Not that I've ever pushed a . . .*

He stirred slightly – and the pain returned in a red rush. All the bleary happiness had gone. Only the sharp horror was left.

I fell out of the sky – my Com was screaming – Mayday, Mayday – this is all wrong – I have to get out of here – this isn't right –

Then someone was standing over him, blocking the light.

It was the young woman. He remembered there'd been a young woman.

'Who are you? I . . . I shouldn't be here . . .' he croaked. 'Where am I? *I have to leave!*' He tried to sit up but she pushed him down again, carefully but firmly. 'How long . . . have I been here?'

She didn't answer. She put her hand on his forehead,

nodded to herself, and then went over into the darkness. He heard a clinking of pottery, as if things were being mixed in a cup. And then she did speak, and he found her voice was already familiar to him. A comforting sound. 'We brought you here when you came out of the sea. Can you understand me now? You were talking seal at first – I wasn't sure you were going to find your way into your human mind. It's a good thing your people are strong. Here, drink this.'

She came out of the darkness, supported his head and held the cup to his mouth. It was bitter. It tasted familiar, as if he'd drunk it before. Then she laid him down again and covered him up.

'What's wrong with me?' He was ashamed to hear how his voice quivered. His eyes filled up with tears.

She made shushing sounds. 'You've been ill. It'll take time to get your strength back. I know you like to bask – I'll get you into the sun soon – but look, see? Today I opened the roof.' She pointed up over her shoulder and gave him an encouraging grin.

She's got a nice smile, thought Rab blearily. *I like her smile.*

Then he was asleep again.

Cait: Skara Brae

He can't die.

And . . .

It'll be your fault if he dies.

Voy hadn't said that, not exactly, but the Old Woman always blamed Cait for everything bad that happened. This would be no different. Besides, it *was* her fault. She was the one who'd found the selkie. She was the one who'd had him brought back to the village. She was the one who could never leave well enough alone.

The burn on the selkie's arm blistered and wept and refused to scab over. And the fever eased and then worsened again . . . did it have something to do with the tides? . . . There was so much she didn't know about the way selkie bodies worked.

Even knowing what to feed him was difficult. She experimented with bits of raw fish and limpets fresh from the seawater storage tank in the corner, trying to push morsels into his mouth. But he only spat them out, wrinkling his nose and making retching noises. It was better when she made them into soup in a clay pot on the embers, and offered him the broth on a horn spoon. He still pulled a disgusted face, but at least he swallowed.

Who would have thought it? She couldn't imagine how his people managed to make soup underwater, but then she couldn't imagine how his people lived at all. She'd seen seals hauled out on the rocks or bobbing curiously close to shore to watch whatever the villagers might be doing, but what they did when they were under the waves was a mystery. Sketh and the other village hunters speared them when they could. Seal skins made excellent clothing, and because of Voy's status as Old Woman, they always got the best pelts and the tastiest cuts of meat . . .

She felt suddenly queasy. Had she inadvertently eaten someone like *him*?! But she pushed the thought away. Not every seal was one of the Fey, just as not every green hump in the ground housed a trow. Besides, no selkie would let an idiot like Sketh skewer him.

Her selkie had pushed aside the covers again, and she looked at him curiously. He was . . . odd. She stroked the skin on his chest lightly. It was quite hairless, even though the selkie was the height and build of a grown man. It was remarkably soft as well and unmarked by scars. And he was the same warm brown colour all over, including the parts that would normally be covered by clothes. But of course seals didn't wear clothes. When they basked in the sun they obviously took care to bake evenly.

Brown like deep, rich earth, except for the palms of his hands and the soles of his feet.

Cait tried to picture how the selkie's human form could be packed inside its seal form – was it like a baby inside its mother? All curled up into a bundle? She shook her head. A man this size, folded up inside the body of a seal? Impossible!

'It would explain why your people wail like that, though!' she whispered to the unconscious selkie.

If that's what he was . . .

She sat back on her heels and chewed her lip. The fire that broke out on his arm, and wounded him so deeply – she'd never heard of that before, in any of the stories.

And then there was the fact that before she saw him sprawling in the shallows, she'd heard something falling. Or she thought she had.

She'd told no one about the plunge into the sea. She'd pushed it to the back of her mind. It was more likely some sea creature breaching in the bay, and the sound being made greater, stranger, by the fog.

If the young man in her bed was a selkie, what could he possibly have been doing in the sky? If not a selkie, then what? What fell from the sky must first fly in the sky, and what, other than birds, could . . .

Her throat went tight and cold.

A lost soul.

There had been whispers about them, more and more as the years went by and the times showed no sign of getting better. They were spirits of humans who, for whatever reason, were not secured before they could be sent on the Road to the Sun. Or, somehow, got lost on that path once started. They were drawn back to places where there was warmth, or where there had been warmth at some time in their past. They haunted villages. They took the breath from babies. They blighted crops. If a burial cairn wasn't properly sealed by stone and fire and water and air, they found their way in, disturbing the bones of the dead. Some people said you could hear them shrieking and moaning in the wind.

For years, the warmth of the Sun had been getting less. Were the souls the Old Women sent from the Ring of Stones not finding their way to Her? Was She giving life and not getting life back again? Was She bleeding to death?

Cait looked in horror at the young man.

34

Is that what he is? A lost soul?

He sighed. His breath smelled of fish broth. Cait felt something unknot inside her. She was pretty certain that wasn't the smell of the afterlife.

No, he was her selkie, sure enough. Could seals fly then? Would that be any stranger than turning into a man? Did they unfurl wings when no one was looking and transform themselves into great sea birds?

If I could do that – if I could fly – I wouldn't be trapped here – water would make no obstacle, or mountains or savage strangers. I would fly to my real home and rouse my people to return here and free what is theirs. I could even fly to the Sun and find out what ails Her. Save the world! They'd sing songs and tell stories about that!

She only realised she'd been smiling when the sharp smell of the selkie wetting himself made her wrinkle up her nose. *Nobody sings songs about piss,* she told herself with a shrug, and began cleaning him up again.

Rab: Skara Brae

He wandered in dreams, searching for something, always searching – *Where are you? Don't leave me here! Don't leave me alone!* – but each time, when he woke, the young woman was there. Her name was Cait. He knew there was someone else – an old woman – living in the hut, but she came and went. It was better when she wasn't there. He hated the way she smelled. He had trouble finding words to describe it, but why should he have lots of words for somebody's stink? At home, people didn't smell at all.

This isn't home, and it isn't a vid, and I haven't had a chance to sanitize in so long, and . . .

And then he would start to cry again.

He hated that. By rights he should be furious, not weeping like a pathetic baby. It was somebody's – something's – fault that he was trapped in this hole, wherever it was – *nobody* deserved to be treated like this – it wasn't fair – not fair –

But he found that anger took energy he just didn't have.

'How long have I been ill?'

Cait shrugged. 'Since you arrived.'

'But how many days has it been? Weeks?'

She shrugged again. She did that a lot.

He'd been asleep again. It was dark, and there was a light now, coming from the back of the hut. He squinted at it and could just make out a bowl, sitting on the stone shelving, with a low flame flickering above it. The young woman must have seen he was stirring. She appeared from the gloom, picked the bowl up and carried it carefully over to the bed box. When she held the light close to his face the whiff of fishy oil caught at the back of his throat and made him cough. He could see the liquid sloshing back and forth, the floating wick drifting about, the light reflecting off the oily sheen.

What kind of place was he lost in, that was so primitive they didn't have proper lights?

He tried to make his brain work. He knew – of course he knew! – that he wasn't where he was supposed to be. *This* wasn't his world. And yet the horrible, terrifying thing was that the world he remembered, the one he *called* his, no longer seemed completely real. It was as if his illness had divided him from it. The things that felt most real to him now were bad things, pain and fever and weakness, but also small, intense pleasures – the taste of cold water, warmth from the coverings on his crude bed, the smell of whatever the soup was she fed him – and her.

Cait.

When all the possibilities of the great wide world seemed to have narrowed down to almost nothing, she was still there.

Cait: Skara Brae

Cait was keeping the selkie alive by guesswork, but there were things about him that worked in his favour. For example, he'd started out fatter than anyone in the village. Probably than anyone on the islands, especially these last years. Life under the water was clearly much easier than life on land. His flesh was firm and his ribs barely showed. He had all his teeth. His earthy brown human skin was soft to the touch, unmarked except for the one burn. When he opened his eyes, they were a deep, dark brown as well, not blue or green or gray. They were liquid and lovely, like all seal eyes. She tried to picture him when he was in his seal form, with those eyes open and a set of stiff whiskers raying out from his cheeks . . .

Suddenly Voy was peering over Cait's shoulder. 'Not dead yet, then.'

'No.'

'And speaking sense?'

Cait shrugged. 'Sometimes.'

'He seems pretty stupid. Still, he'll be fit for coupling one of these fine days, and no one needs to be smart for that. Don't tell me you haven't been thinking of it.'

Cait didn't look up. Voy was baiting her. Best act stupid herself.

Hissing her sneering laugh, the Old Woman left them alone.

Rab: Skara Brae

Then a time came when Rab woke – and the pain was less.

It felt like the middle of the night. *Though how would I know?* The flaps of hide from the canopy over the bed had been dropped down. Moving with elaborate care, he reached over and pushed one aside. He looked into the room, dimly lit by the embers in the hearth and saw her, Cait, curled up asleep on the hard, cold ground.

He wondered idly why she slept there. It didn't occur to him it was because he had taken her bed.

He heard steady snores coming from the other stone bed box. So the old woman was there too.

He was immensely tired, but the main thing, the thing he really cared about, was the pain being less. Becoming something he could almost detach himself from.

He rested his chin on the stone side and stared at the fire. He'd seen simulations of open fires before, in historical reconstructions at museums. One of his lecturers had been particularly keen on stuff like that. *'Recapturing the feel of the time. The ambience.'* But the simulations had been a million miles off. He knew that now. Too clean. Too odour-less. Two-dimensional. Real fires spat and filled the room with smoke that stung your eyes and throat. Real fires mesmerized.

You could stare at a fire for ages.

He stared.

It had died down now, but then a bit of fuel shifted and

a single flame flared up. It illuminated the tall driftwood stick leaning against the old woman's bed. The light reflected on the polished surface of the wood, the long twisted shaft, the curious shape at the top.

That's not firewood, he thought. *That's a real wizard's staff, or maybe that should be witch ...* He frowned, trying to remember his reading on early belief systems. *A witch's staff ... or broomstick ... it's broomsticks for witches ... or have I got that muddled ...?*

But he didn't need to know what kind of stick it was to know the old woman was powerful. It surrounded her, coming off her as strong as her smell.

'You don't need to be pretty to have charisma.' Who'd said that? He couldn't remember, but it was clearly true. The old woman might be bent and wrecked-looking and badly in need of sanitising, but it didn't change a thing.

She was the one in charge.

The peace he had felt on waking began to drain away.

What kind of place is this? How am I going to get home?

He lay back, letting the hide curtain drop back into place. For the first time he didn't fall asleep immediately. For a long while he stared up with dry, burning eyes at the alien dark.

How am I going to get home?

Threaded through his fevered awareness were the sounds of people, from beyond the walls of this hut – the shouts of children, babies crying, adults calling back and forth to each other, muffled but somewhere nearby. From time to time there were odd scratching noises and Cait would go and crouch at the low doorway and murmur quietly with

40

unseen visitors. Sometimes she would fetch something for them from the stone shelves, but they never came in, or lingered.

Cait and the old woman were the only people he saw, and yet he was aware of others all around. Just like at home.

Not like home at all.

The waking times gradually grew longer.

Sometimes the old woman was there when Rab opened his eyes. Voy was her name. She had a way of sitting and staring at him, not blinking, as if he were something that might be edible.

Cait barely spoke to him if Voy was there. He found himself rather desperately trying to catch her eye during these times. But it was as if she'd gone way down inside herself where he couldn't reach her.

Once when Cait was helping him back from the toilet alcove, he whispered to her, 'Who *is* she? Is she your mother?'

Cait pulled away from him so abruptly he almost fell to the ground. Her eyes were furious, but before she could say anything they both heard the old woman's hissing, sniggering laugh.

'That's right. I gave her life. That makes me her mother, wouldn't you say? Wouldn't you say, girl?'

Cait's fingers hurt him as she helped him back into bed.

'My mother's dead.' Her voice was flat and expressionless.

The mostly unconscious place in his head where his own mother was lodged suddenly leapt into focus. It hurt to think of her, so he pushed the thought away.

41

Meanwhile, Voy went on hissing to herself, though Rab couldn't understand what she was laughing about.

There were so many things he didn't understand.

And then, late one afternoon, he woke to find his brain clear. It was the strangest sensation – light and cold and detached. Instead of the horrible jumble of feelings and fragments and shapeless fears, he felt he might at last have an instrument he could use. He'd almost forgotten what that was like.

Where am I? No, that's not right, because the suit only moves in time, not in space. He was pleased with himself for remembering that. *So, WHEN am I? That's what I need to know.*

He thought about the little information he had to go on. Where to start . . . The malfunction had happened in the 19th century. Victorian Age. First Industrial Revolution. Steam power. Birth of archaeology.

Not like *this*. And none of the history he'd learned covering the period between then and his own time was anything like this either, was it? Not even during the worst days of the Nadir had things been so bad, so debased, that people had to live without even rudimentary electricity.

So he must have gone even further back, even earlier than the 19th century.

How far back?

What did he know that would narrow things down? He'd been nowhere but in the sea, on the shore and inside this hut so far – *and out of my head most of the time*. He didn't have to look around to remind himself – everything in the place was as clear to him as if it were incised on the

42

inside of his eyelids. The square hearth, the bed boxes, the stone shelving against the wall. On the wall opposite that, the low, square door. Animal hides – on the beds, over the beds as canopies, made into clothes. Fleeces and felted materials. As far as he could tell, fire was their only power source. These were a primitive people, pre-industrial by a long shot. Now that he thought about it, had he seen anything made of any kind of metal about the place? Pots? Knives?

Nothing. *Unless metal was just for men . . .* He'd only seen the two women so far and historically there were all sorts of distinctions between the genders – he'd had a whole series of lectures on that. But then he remembered one of *these* women was Voy. He shook his head. Nobody was going to tell *her* she couldn't have something.

So no metal . . . Just how far do you have to go back in time to get to people who only have stone to work with, and clay, and bits of bone . . .

The Bone Age? No, it wasn't called that . . .

The Stone Age.

'You're awake?' It was Cait. She was crouched by the bed box, looking at him. 'How are you feeling? You look a bit strange.'

Is that possible? Could I have been thrown so far back? Isn't there some kind of limit on time-travelling technology? He couldn't remember. His mind was starting to drown in panic all over again.

'Here, drink this.'

'NO!' he shouted, pushing the cup away so hard the contents splashed up into Cait's face. 'No more drugs! You can't keep drugging me! I have to be able to think!'

Cait wiped the liquid from her cheek. 'It's water,' she

43

said. 'That's all. You're human now, so you need to drink.'

What does she mean, 'You're human now'? Scut – if she thinks I'm human now, what did she think I was before?

Remember the lectures . . .

Before World Unification, he'd been taught, different groups of people each felt that they were proper humans, and that the members of other groups were . . . something else. Lesser. His lecturer had said this was a defining feature of Earth history. Some of the groupings were geographical, some religious, some based on gender or sexual orientation or racial characteristics. There had been all sorts of rules against inter-breeding – before the Alexander Decision, sex had preoccupied his ancestors to an extraordinary degree. Rab remembered thinking how odd it was that they could be so *interested* and yet not understand how stupid the fetish about purity was. How long it had taken them to understand that humans came out best, the more genetically mixed they were.

That could be it. She could think I'm from some other tribe, a not-quite-human-because-it's-not-hers tribe. But now for some reason I've maybe been awarded honorary human-ness.

Just because it was stupid didn't mean it wasn't true. If he was right, and this was the Stone Age, what other sorts of things might they believe in?

And then something horrible erupted in his mind.

If technology to them meant bashing rocks with other rocks, what would they think of the Time Wender – his Silver Skin?

Sudden sweat trickled down his back. It was his only

way home, and they might not even have noticed it. They might have left it to be washed out to sea. Or they might have destroyed it . . . it might be gone forever . . .

He tried to clear his throat. 'When you found me, was there, you know, anything *with* me? Any sort of, um, clothes?'

She shook her head. 'No clothes.'

Red crept up his neck, as he tried not to think of the number of times she must have seen him naked. *Concentrate, Rab – this is important!*

'Are you sure? It wouldn't have looked like the kind of clothes I'm wearing now. It was a suit, like—' he tried to make shapes with his hands '—and it was shiny. And silver?'

She let her pale hair fall forward over her face. 'You mean your skin.'

'Yes – that's it – the Skin – the Silver Skin.' It didn't occur to him to wonder how she knew its name. 'Where is it?' He tried to sound casual, but when she turned away without answering he couldn't stop his voice from cracking. 'WHERE IS IT? I need the suit – I mean, the skin – I need it back!' Tears pricked hotly at his eyes. It might be too damaged to take him back but he might still be able to use it to send a message. 'It might help me, you see. Help me to talk to my people – I need to tell them I'm all right – I'm not dead!'

He stopped, appalled at the words he'd not even clearly thought before.

What if they think I'm dead?

Eventually that was what they *would* think. They'd think he was dead and they'd stop looking for him and he'd be trapped here forever. And then he'd grow older and older until it *would* be true, because he'd die here, in this awful hole, surrounded by stinking savages who didn't know anything about anything. He'd be dead and in the real world – *his* world – *his* time – they'd forget all about him. It would be as if he'd never lived. *Even though, all the time, I'd be right here.*

All the time. The words didn't make any sense any more.

Nothing made sense any more.

They'd be looking for him – of course they would. He was only supposed to be away for two hours. Then, when he didn't come back, his mother would start to worry. And then she'd start to panic. She'd raise the alarm, and they'd start looking . . . but they'd be looking in the wrong place – no, not place, *time* – the wrong *time*. He was lost in time, and that was so much bigger than even the whole world. *Grain of sand on a beach . . . grain of sand . . .*

That was all he was now.

Without help, they would never find him.

Unless I can let them know I'm here. Unless I can get hold of the suit and activate my Com and send them my location. I've got to get the suit back.

He tried to turn back the wave of fear that threatened to engulf him. He tried to not think about the fire. He tried to not think about the malfunction or how badly damaged his Com might be.

If I can just get my hands on the suit, everything will be all right . . .

His head hurt and when the hot tears came he found he hadn't the strength to wipe them away.

Cait brought another cup. 'This isn't water,' she said.

'Thank you,' Rab said humbly. He took it and, in spite of the bitter taste, drained it dry.

Just before dawn, he woke again. The pain in his arm had worsened. He gritted his teeth and tried not to move, but he couldn't help a whimper escaping. The Old Woman's snoring filled the room, but Cait heard him. She knelt by the bed and took his arm in her hands.

'This needs re-dressing. It will hurt. Try to think about something else.'

There was only one thing *to* think about. Getting away. Getting home.

Break it down, Rab. One step at a time.

How had he got here, in the first place?

What actually happened, back there, in the sky? It was hard to remember – it seemed so long ago – *scut*, it felt like forever. Not knowing what time it was, what day, what week – it made him want to scream. He pushed the panic away and tried to concentrate.

What went wrong?

There had been the brief visit to the Deluvian, but his Com had seemed completely at ease, and there'd been no hint of a Silver Skin malfunction . . .

He shook his head. *It was after. It was when we tried to get to the 19th-century date. To 1850.*

He'd assumed that the noise and the blinding light had been a part of the suit malfunctioning, but what if they had been what had *caused* the malfunction?

Think about when you were then. Victorian Age. Long before Cloud Control.

He dredged up from his memory the lectures on rogue weather. They'd put a lot of emphasis on how

47

much earlier ages were at the mercy of meteorological events. It was hard to imagine a world where rain, wind, thunderstorms, hurricanes, all happened at random, and where trying to guess what might come next was the best anyone could do.

Cloud Control had been an essential science, developing concurrently with the original housing stack designs. Otherwise the towers would have been under frequent, deadly lightning attack as the tallest structures in the landscape.

What if that was it? What if I was struck by wild lightning?

The suit's first priority would be to protect him. The next would be to protect his Com. In the split-second of a lightning strike, it would have automatically focused all power on defence – making itself not be there in a different way to the way it hadn't been there before . . . Rab groaned. He'd *never* understood quantum relevance. He tried desperately to dig through half-remembered and never-entirely-digested equations and expositions.

Maybe the combination of the lightning's power and its own quantum activities had thrown him sideways wildly into the past – not sideways, exactly, but whatever the temporal equivalent of sideways was – short circuiting, unless it was *over* circuiting he meant, the fine tuning. Some almost infinitesimal linking to the time he'd ended up in must exist, or maybe this was just as far as the suit got before it completely conked out. In which case he should be grateful the Silver Skin hadn't carried him any *further* back. There were worse things he could have been facing now than bad smells and too much fish to eat.

Dinosaurs ... primordial ooze ... nothing but lava and volcanic ash ... Rab shuddered. He was lucky to arrive when there was air to breathe.

So. Best guess: he'd been hit by lightning. Next question: what kind of havoc did something as powerful as lightning wreak?

All kinds. He had to face it. There was every chance his Com was dead. And if it wasn't, even if it was just damaged, what made him think he could fix it? He didn't know the first thing about fixing Coms. At home, they had Coms to do that.

Think, Rab, think! Stop focusing on all the things you don't know – what DO you know?

He frowned. He was getting a headache and the skin of his injured arm was pulsing again, objecting to Cait's handling.

Skin . . .

What had his Com said? *It draws energy from your specific electrical field ...* That's why he'd had to strip off, all that time ago, in his bedroom. It needed to be in contact with his skin to draw power. Maybe, just maybe, that was all it needed. An energy source. Him, in fact. If he could just get his hands on it, put it on again, maybe that was all he had to do. Give it some juice and maybe it would repair *itself* . . .

Maybe getting away from this hole was going to be simpler than he'd feared.

All he had to do was get himself and his suit together again.

'There. Go back to sleep.'

Cait had finished dressing the burn and was gathering up her pots and pastes. He had to ask her *now*.

'Where is it?' he whispered to Cait, grabbing her arm to keep her from leaving him. 'Where's my skin?'

She froze for an instant, then gently extracted herself from his clutch. At first he thought she wasn't going to answer, but then she moved her eyes deliberately, slowly, towards the bed box on the other side of the room, and then back to him. Rab raised his eyebrows and she gave the barest nod.

'I'm sorry.' She breathed the words but he didn't hear her. He had already lain back, his heart pounding.

I know where it is! he thought to himself. *I know where it is.*

Cait: Skara Brae

Cait was restless. As she went about the first of the day's tasks, she could hear the wind in the thatch. It would be good down on the shore this morning. Salt-tasting wind and waves and sky – they would help clear away all the sick-room smells that had been filling her head for so long. They were what she needed.

Maybe she'd even have time to go to her cave. It had been too long.

Voy had left already, at daybreak, without a word. And, after another broken night, the selkie now seemed to be sleeping soundly.

That's right – you sleep. It will do you good. Help you heal. Tomorrow I'll get you out in the sun. Or maybe even later today. I think you're almost ready.

She opened the roof window to let in the air. Then she ducked out into the passage, shutting the door behind her and putting the bar across, so no one would come scratching and disturb his peace. And she put him out of her mind.

Rab: Skara Brae

He didn't know how long he had slept.

He'd lain still, as if asleep, even though his nose itched and he could feel a cramp coming in his left leg, until, finally, Cait finished pottering about the place and left. He waited for a long moment, to be sure she wasn't going to suddenly remember something and come back . . . No. She was gone.

He got up too fast and had to grab the edge of the bed for a moment till the sparkling lights cleared from his eyes. He breathed deeply, looked to the head of the hearth, where the Old Woman's seat waited with its mantle of fur. At the stone shelves behind it, stacked with clay pots, nameless bits of bone and rock, rolled-up animal skins. At the weird little carved rock things. Anywhere but at his goal.

Hurry up – what's the matter with you? Go ON!

He forced his foot to edge forward – and then his heart leapt into his throat at a sudden scream overhead.

His knees went weak and he cursed out loud, but it was only a gull – he could see it through the hole in the roof, high over the village, a white shape in the blue. *Just a stupid bird.* It couldn't see him, down here in the dark. It didn't know what he was doing.

You're not doing ANYTHING, you idiot! Get ON!

He staggered round the hearth in an awkward rush and stopped short by the old woman's bed. There were carved marks on the edge of the stone side – they leapt out at him, menacing in a way scratches on rock had no right to be. *Get a grip, Rab!* He made himself lean across the marks.

He was sweating as he reached into the bed box and started to search.

Cait: Skara Brae

Old Benth had caught Cait at the entrance to the paved place. They were always after her for the small things, especially since Gairstay, the Old Chert, had died, and Voy had become even more angry and unapproachable. But at last Cait managed to extract herself from the ancient woman's toothless complaints. She settled the gathering bag on her shoulder and started out for the shore with a determined stride when . . .

'Cait? Your pardon, but if I could speak with you for one small moment only . . .?'

Pretend you didn't hear – just keep walking – you've got long legs – just casually speed up –

'Cait? Cait? Your pardon?'

Cait sighed. It was Mewie, using her most gentle, most humble voice, which pretty much meant exactly the opposite. Whatever it was she was after – probably more of the rash balm for Mot – she would go on about it, in that soft, mild voice, on and on and on until she got what she wanted.

Cait fought the urge to turn and snarl at her – *What are you going to do when I'm gone? Eh? When there's only Voy to face with all your little issues and aches? What are you going to do then?*

She'd been close to doing that a hundred times, but this time she had to bite her tongue in earnest. There was no getting around it – the selkie had unsettled her. Somehow he was stirring up all the longings she'd managed to keep in check, waiting till the moment when Voy would finally relent – would finally give her the words she needed – and she'd be able to leave. Not just an escape to the shore for a few hours, but properly. Completely.

However, until she gave Mewie what *she* wanted, there would be no going *anywhere*.

With a sigh, she turned.

Rab: Skara Brae

It has to be here – it has to be –

He'd started so carefully, delicately feeling among the coverings, laying them aside one by one – but now there was none of that. Now he was ripping out the heather and bracken bedding in desperate handfuls, peering at each in the pool of light from the roof hole, before casting them aside wildly. In his panic he couldn't even remember what the Skin looked like – he found himself wasting time scrabbling through clumps of vegetation that could barely conceal an arm or leg, let alone the whole suit.

Still no sign.

He leaned right over the edge of the front slab, feeling into every corner with his one good hand, bruising his fingers on the cold stone.

'Nothing! Nothing!' he panted, scrabbling in the empty space, refusing to believe what his eyes were telling him – one last sweep – and then . . . something. He felt something.

A notch in the floor stone.

He could slide his fingers in. His thoughts had gone all sharp and still. *There must be a hollow underneath the floor.* It was awkward, but he tensed his good arm and heaved – and there was a definite shift. The flagstone lifted, just a little.

He sat back on his heels. *Light. I need better light.* He went to the shelves and brought one of the fish oil lamps to light from the embers of the fire, the way he'd seen

Cait do. *I can't hold the lamp and lift the slab at the same time, not with just one good arm.* He balanced the lamp precariously on the front corner of the bed box. It didn't help much – mostly it cast shadows and made him squint, but he flexed his fingers and leaned into the bed box once more.

The stone moved. But it was heavy and hard to raise from such an awkward angle. He gritted his teeth and ignored the way his fingers cracked, and slowly, slowly, the edge of the slab began to lift. Higher and higher, until he had to pause to shift his grip a little, and realised he could see through the gap into a black space beneath.

It wasn't empty. There was something – if only he had a decent light. He tried to see, his arm muscles shaking with the strain. It was hard to get a sense of size since he couldn't tell how deep the hiding place was, but there was something pale – white, or silvery – something like the fingers of a glove – he craned over, peered closer – but it wasn't a glove – there were fingers all right but they were not cloth or metal or the material of the suit.

They were bones.

With a shriek, he let go of the stone slab – it crashed down with a hollow boom – the lamp overbalanced and smashed into the bed box –

'*What are you doing?!*'

He was no longer alone. Cait was there, paused in the doorway, half in, half out. Before he could speak, she rushed forward, tackled him, crashed on top of him on the floor – she hit him in the face and then, gripping her two hands agonizingly around his throat, she began to squeeze.

PART TWO

PART TWO

Voy: North of Skara Brae

It would be windy and wild up on the headland above the bay. That suited Voy.

The wind kept the attacks of blankness off. If she sat still too long in the warm dimness of her house, they could creep up on her unawares. Then she would come to suddenly, not sure how much time had passed, a bit of dribble on her chin. Tired. So tired. If she caught Cait looking at her oddly then it took all her will to act as if everything was normal.

So she sought the wind. At daybreak, she left the village and climbed to the chambered cairn on the north headland to be with Gairstay. She still preferred the company of his white bones to that of any living person. His were laid in the cairn, with those of the other villagers who had gone back to the Sun, but his spirit hadn't made the journey yet. Each cycle, she and the Old Women of the other villages led the processions inland to the Ring of Hills and the Ring of Stones within it. Each village presented their offerings on the great square hearth. The spirits of the dead, held safe in the carved stones, were brought out, ready to be set free on the Road back to the Source. But at too many of the last cycles, the Sun had stayed sulky behind clouds, and there'd been nothing to do but bring the spirit stones home again.

The world was changing. The dark days seemed to never leave.

She was panting and everything ached by the time she reached the top of the headland and started along the path to where the cairn clung to the seaward edge. She dragged her hair out of her eyes and looked out over the bay. Another new section had fallen away from the cliff face of the southern headland opposite, leaving a raw gash of lighter coloured rock, and a pile of ragged rubble at its foot.

The sea ate cliffs. Someday it would eat so much of this headland that the domed cairn and the bones of the people would fall away into the waves. The ones who built the cairn there so many generations ago must have had that in mind. It must have been part of the plan, if only anyone remembered. Someone once knew the reason – and the response – but that someone died at some point along the way before they passed their knowledge on. It happened. Painfully often. And then no one knew.

Was it meant to be a sign? When the cairn fell into the sea would that mean they should immediately do . . . something? Leave? Stay? Change their ways?

What would the world look like then?

She was doing it again. She frowned as she reached the cairn and laid her stick aside to slide down clumsily by the entrance. (She didn't go inside. She'd seen to it the place was sealed by stone and fire and water and air. No ghoul was going to be sniffing round *her* man!) She had plenty that needed thinking about in the here and now and yet her thoughts drifted away to the future or the past and refused to stay settled in the present. *Old people wander, but I am not old. Not yet. I CHOOSE to think these thoughts.*

The sea was mighty, down in the bay. Great grey waves

came all the way from where the sky met the water, to thunder onto the sands and batter at the cliffs.

It was wild that day too – do you remember, Gairstay? All day the sea kept throwing itself at the beach and the cliffs, so high into the air you'd have thought it would splash the sky. You could taste the salt on your lips as far inland as the village, probably further. It was fierce, that sea, grey and hungry, but I don't remember feeling anything special about the day, anything out of the ordinary. An angry sea. She snorted. *I'd be more likely to notice a peaceful one!* She rubbed her face with a twisted hand and shook her head. *I still don't know why I went out that night. Oh, afterwards I took credit. Of course I did. But at the time, all I know is, somewhere in the middle of the night, I got up and went down to the beach. I remember the moon was near full, with the clouds still racing by, ripped and ragged and the light pouring through them and dimming and pouring through again, and there she was. Just a shape, rolling in the surf. I remember thinking, 'Seal? Beached dolphin? What is that?' Even after I'd dragged her out of the reach of the water I couldn't quite believe my eyes.*

It was a woman. With a nine-month belly that was knotting and taut when Voy put her hand to it. She must have fallen from an Offlander boat. Or maybe the boat had foundered and she was the only one who survived. There was no way of knowing.

I was strong in those days – do you remember? – but carrying her was a hard night's work, I'm telling you. By the time I got her up to the village I was nearly spent, and she – she was screaming and everyone else thought she was something uncanny and hid under their sleeping

63

furs. Everyone except you. You came rushing out with a knife in your hand.

They'd had need of that knife before the night was through. By the time the sun came up the woman was dead, with her belly cut open from hip to chest, and nothing left of her but a mewling bundle, and a promise.

At least Voy was pretty sure there'd been a promise.

In between bouts of screaming, the woman had talked. If you could call it that. She used words that were strange, but there were gestures it wasn't hard to understand – gestures for *Help me! Save my baby!* And towards the end – *Forget me – only save my baby! Please, please . . . promise me . . .*

And she did. She promised, by gesture and word, that she would do as the dying woman asked. Of course she promised. Things were bad enough with the village without adding an unhappy spirit to blight the crops, make the hearth fires spit and smoke, block up the drainage passages from the latrines with stink and disease – there was no end to the trouble lost souls could inflict, left to their own devices.

Of course she promised, ignoring the *Be careful!* messages Gairstay was sending her across the woman's body. Ignoring her own doubts, until it was too late.

'What will you do now?' he'd asked as she wiped the blood off the protesting baby.

'Raise it.' She'd checked between the baby's legs. 'Raise her. Misha has milk enough for her as well as her own, and I'll do the rest . . .'

He'd lifted his eyebrows at her, in that way that used to make her so mad.

'You think I can't?!'

64

She'd seen the other women – *how hard could it be?* She'd pushed away the feeling of terrified inadequacy with anger. That always worked.

But that wasn't what he'd been asking.

'What will you do with HER?' It was the mother he'd meant. 'You can't put her in the cairn. She doesn't belong. I'm not even sure you can hold her spirit in a stone – who knows how strong she is? Her people – assuming she *is* an Offlander – may use some completely different way of protecting themselves, and even if we knew what it was . . .'

He shook his head.

'What if sending her spirit on the Road meant the Sun would shine more strongly on whatever lands *she* came from? What if it meant She looked away from us even more?'

Voy hadn't thought of that. It was a danger, truly.

He looked across at her. He was worried. He was out of his depth. She was too, but she couldn't let anyone see that. She couldn't even let him see it. For all their closeness, he needed her to know what to do, just as much as any of the others did.

Know what to do, or else act as if you did. That was how it was.

She looked down at the dead woman's face. Her skin was strange and her eyes, closed now, had been milky blue, like a blind person's, though Voy could swear she saw out of them well enough. Her long pale hair had dried now so that the unnatural colour showed clearly, even through the encrusting salt. Voy touched it gently.

'If you only saw her hair you'd think she was old. But she's not. She's younger than us, Gairstay.'

65

'Is she – was she . . . normal? Those eyes . . .'

Voy had thought for a while. She'd had experience of some of the ways things could go wrong. There had been that child who came to the Ring of Stones a few cycles in a row, from one of the more northerly villages. It had had even paler skin than this woman's and colourless hair, and its eyes had been colourless too, except for the red rims. Everyone had thought it was a trow changeling, making the sign against evil whenever they saw it, but the mother clung to it nevertheless. And then one year Voy didn't see it at the Ring.

Nothing was said. Children who were abnormal rarely lasted to bear children of their own. Either they withered and died young, or the village stepped in.

But the woman she'd found on the shore hadn't seemed like that.

'Maybe she was normal for her people. Maybe we look stunted and dark to her.'

Gairstay said, 'We may be stunted, but our women bear their babies without having to have them cut out of them.'

But Voy shook her head. 'The baby was the wrong way round – she didn't have a chance. I've seen this before – it can happen to our women too. A baby that comes out butt first is almost always dead. The mothers die too, or if they live they often don't heal easily or well. Cutting a baby like that out is the only way to save it.'

Gairstay looked uneasy. These were women's mysteries, and he'd already seen more of such things this night than was good. He went back to the practicalities.

'What are we going to do with the body?'

Voy didn't answer for a long time. Over their heads the

tag end of the wind howled and died away, howled and died. In the silences he could hear the surf booming onto the beach. The villagers would be staying close indoors today as much as they could. His mind wandered to the lump of flint he'd been saving up for just such an indoor day. He'd felt its awkwardness – and the fine blade within – and he knew it would take all his concentration to chip away just the right slivers –

'Let the girl decide.' Voy's voice broke abruptly through his thoughts.

'What?'

'When she's grown into whatever she's to grow into, then I'll let her decide what to do with her mother. Till then,' she'd said blithely all that time ago, 'I'll keep the spirit safe, and us safe from it . . .'

They'd done it together. And told the villagers the next day that the baby in the Old Woman's arms was here to stay.

'She's human,' Voy told them. 'Offlander. I have examined her and she is not of the Fey.'

She knew that wouldn't stop the whispering and the wondering. But as long as nothing much changed, they'd get used to the girl. Forget there had ever been anything strange in her arrival. And nothing much *had* changed. (Except for the girl growing taller than Sketh. Voy enjoyed how cross that made him!) The weather went on being bad. The crops went on being poor. More times than not, when they made the journey to the Ring, no Road opened. The Sun didn't appear. She skulked behind clouds and rain and refused to show Herself, no matter how hard they asked – begged – for blessing.

What kind of sickness could have infected Her, that

She refused to be cured by the return of good souls – fed by Her own loving people? Did She *wish* to die?

The way Gairstay had?

Voy shut her eyes tight. She couldn't think about that. She couldn't *not* think about that. The picture of him filled her mind, the picture of him as he stopped eating, stopped drinking, grew gaunt and grim and eager to leave her behind. Leave the pain behind. It had only been a matter of time. Choosing the time yourself was sometimes the only choice, when there wasn't any choice at all. She knew all that, but it didn't help.

It was never the plan for you to die first, you coward. What am I to do without you? Tell me that, why don't you.

She pounded at the turf with her useless hands but there was no answer.

And now there's another mystery, spat out by the sea, for me to deal with. And a fat lot of help you are to me now!

It was time to go back. Pick up the burden of them all, with no one to share it.

Cold to her twisted bones, Voy made herself stand up.

Time to find out what my two gobbets of sea spew are up to . . .

Cait: Skara Brae

The rage came up from Cait's belly like sick.

'*What have you done – what have you done*—' She gripped his throat tighter and tighter, ignoring the way his brown eyes pleaded and bulged, his skin suffused, his fingers clawed desperately at her.

'CAIT!'

Out of nowhere, the Old Woman was there, looming over them, seeming to swell until her head must have brushed the roof beams, her shoulders touched the walls. The power coming off her knocked Cait away from Rab so hard she banged the back of her head against the stone side of the bed box. For a moment her vision blurred – when it cleared, Rab was over on the other side of the room making retching, gasping noises, and there was bright red nose blood dripping down his chin. *Good.* She was shaking, appalled that she'd left him alone here, that she'd brought him into the village in the first place, saved his life. How could she have been so stupid?

But look at him! Even now, it didn't show. He was sitting there, pretending to look shocked, and bewildered, and terrified, without even knowing who he was most scared of, for he kept looking back and forth between herself and Voy – back and forth, back and forth, like a baby trying to focus on two things at the same time. It would have been comical if she didn't hate him so much. She pulled her lips back from her teeth, and snarled. Voy slashed at her across the shoulders with her stick but she didn't care about the pain.

Rab shrank against the wall, making snuffling noises. Voy ignored him. She stood there, staring at Cait. Waiting.

Cait glowered and glared, but gradually the red anger died down. Gradually doubt crept in.

How does she know? thought Cait, struggling to keep meeting the Old Woman's eyes. *How does she know I wouldn't be able to keep the anger clear in my mind? How does she always know?*

The Old Woman turned to leave.

'Clean it up,' she said over her shoulder.

And then she was gone again.

Cait stared at the empty doorway. *Is that it? Is that all you're going to say?* She was starting to ache where Voy had hit her, and somehow that made it even harder to stay safe inside the fury. She tried to, anyway.

'If you've hurt her,' she whispered at Rab. 'If you've done anything to her, I'll kill you.' Her words sounded thin and unconvincing, even to herself. It was as if Voy had taken all the energy out of the room with her.

'Done anything to who?' He must have sensed she wasn't going to hit him again. He sat up straighter and started to dab at his face gingerly with his sleeve. He winced. 'What the scut are you talking about? Why did you attack me? And why did you lie – my suit's not there – what's she done with it? I need my suit – don't you *understand*? Without the suit I'll be stuck here forever – I'll be stuck here till I *die* – unless—' A look of horror crossed his face. 'Unless I'm dead already and . . . The accident – was that when I died – and none of this is real – it's just a nightmare – it's some sort of primitive afterlife?'

'Don't be stupid,' Cait snapped. 'Look at the way you're bleeding. The Dead don't bleed.' *Ghouls don't either,* a voice in her head reminded her, and the last shreds of her fury dwindled away.

Rab let out a breath that bubbled blood. 'Yeah. Right. *I'm* stupid. And it's just normal, is it, to go crazy and beat me up for no reason at all?'

'No reason at all? What were you *doing*?'

'Looking for my skin. Where you told me to look. What did you think I was doing?'

'You were . . . what?'

'You told me – last night, with that look, don't you remember? I asked you where my skin was and you *looked*. Over there. At her bed. I thought you were saying my suit, I mean, skin, was in her bed – so I went looking for it.'

'No. No! I meant *she* had it – *Voy* has it – she carries it with her. All the time. Did you think she was going to leave it lying about for you to find? Do you think she doesn't know *anything*?'

'Then what did you think I was doing? What made you go crazy like that?' Before she could answer, he whispered, 'Oh, scut, Cait, I must be losing my mind. Do you know what I thought I saw in there? In a hole, under the bed?'

She looked him straight in the eyes.

'Of course,' she said. 'I know exactly what you saw. You saw my mother.'

Voy: Skara Brae

Voy paused in the passageway. That – in there – that had felt good! She'd been so successful at cowing everyone years ago, she rarely got the chance to flex the muscles of her will any more. She'd almost forgotten how much she enjoyed that sense of . . . what? . . . *inflating*.

Swelling up like a big old frog in spring. She grinned at herself and then shrugged.

Well, it wasn't spring now, and hadn't been for a long time. She'd stopped them from killing each other, though it hadn't looked as if the selkie had been doing much except bleating. Now by rights she should stay and listen, see what she could learn. The reconciliation might be . . . enlightening, and an Old Woman could never know too much. The selkie certainly *looked* like a functioning male, though to match up to what the stories promised he'd have to do a lot more than just look the part.

But the aching was back in her bones and she suddenly couldn't remember when she'd eaten last – and there was a delectable smell coming down the long passageway.

Turning awkwardly, she shuffled off to see what Sidne had in her pot today.

Rab: Skara Brae

'You're telling me there's a corpse under the bed. You're telling me you've got your mother buried right where you've been living – where *I've* been living. What is the *matter* with you – that's – that's—' He felt his voice getting high and squeaky. 'You knew it – you knew she was there – all this time – and then you let me put my *hand* in there . . .'

'I didn't *let* you – it was *your* idea – I thought you must be some kind of ghoul—'

'You think I'm – you thought I was *what*?!'

And then, with a gesture that reminded him suddenly, heartbreakingly, of his own mother, she shuffled over and pushed his head back.

'Hold still. I can't do anything with you until your nose stops bleeding.'

And then she began to talk.

She told him about the First People and the lost souls and the ways of ghouls. And why her mother was buried under the floor with the fifth spirit stone binding her in place. And how she couldn't leave to go looking for her proper people until Voy taught her some magic words to set her mother free. And as she talked, she wiped the blood from his face.

He tried to imagine what it would be like to actually believe this stuff. To feel invisible danger all around. To not know if the next person you met was human or something else entirely that was out to get you, one way

73

or another. When they'd studied the superstitions of early cultures it had never occurred to him just how stressful it would be, just how paranoid it must make you feel. The care and worry that went into all the strange things they did to protect themselves. Against ... nothing. *It's all fairy tales. Including me ...*

She told him how the spirits of the dead had to be held in the carved stones, sometimes for years, before they could be sent back to the sun at some place, a ring of stones somewhere inland. And how their presence in a village, waiting, drew the attention of the ghouls.

She didn't meet his eyes.

She thought I was one of those. He rolled the thought around his mind for a moment like an unfamiliar taste. *Me, the terrifying bad guy. Creature from the dark. Powerful ... scary ...* There was no getting around it – it felt ever so slightly good.

He suddenly realised she'd stopped talking. She must have guessed he'd stopped listening.

Then, 'Well? What do *you* think you are?' she said, her voice husky.

'I can't say.'

She sighed and shrugged. 'That fits with the stories. In the stories about the selkies they say that, in human form, you have no memory of your other life.'

She thinks I mean 'can't say' like 'I can't remember' – not like 'I'm not allowed.' Well, he wasn't going to clear it up for her. Besides, she'd never believe the truth, even if he did break the Non-Intervention Contract. *Break it? I've shattered it a thousand times –*

'Ow!'

74

She gave his face a final wipe, none too gently. 'But if you can't remember what you are, how do you know you're not what *I* thought you are?'

'You *want* to believe I'm a soul-sucking ghoul?'

'I want to believe you're a selkie.' She flung the blood-stained bog cotton across the room and suddenly she was shouting again. 'I want to believe you come from under the sea and maybe you saw what happened to my mother and you can tell me – did she fall? Was she pushed? – and did my father drown? Did the ship founder and no one knew? I want to believe you can take me on your back and swim to the land of my people or if you *can* fly – if I *did* hear you drop out of the sky – I want you to go and find them for me and say, 'Come and take Cait home!' And while you're at it, make the Sun strong again and the crops grow and make Voy teach me the words so I can release my mother. But you can't do any of that, can you? Can you?'

Rab didn't hear her. He couldn't hear anything except the blood pounding in his ears. She was so magnificent, with her pale hair thrown back like that and her eyes blazing and the shape of her body under her clothes and –

Scut! What's the matter with me – going all cave-man – maybe it's something in the water . . .

He choked, as if the sudden realisation was trying to climb out his throat. It wasn't the water. Not *this* water . . .

All citizens were taught about the Alexander Decision and the famous speech that swayed the last dissenters in the World Parliament – 'Never again! Never again!' Nothing had ever worked before – imposed quotas, economic pressures like famine and drought, the decimation of warfare and local violence, pleas to self-control. Humanity in its raw form was a breeding disaster that could not be stopped.

So it was decided to change the raw material. A gentle nudge, no more, in the direction of lowering libido and freeing up all that energy for other things. It didn't stop people fancying each other, and sex was still the best way to make babies, but it was no longer an all-consuming obsession. And all it took was the merest addition to the drinking water – unnoticeable.

Only, Rab wasn't drinking that water any more.

He looked down at his hands with a kind of horror, as if they belonged to someone else. Someone he didn't know. If he stayed here any longer, what could he become? What was he becoming already?

'Rab?'

Cait was standing in front of him, too close, making him too aware of her body and her smell. She tried to take his hands, but he pulled away and staggered back.

'No!'

She kept coming nearer. 'I'm sorry I tried to kill you.'

He grabbed her shoulders, holding her off. 'You don't understand – I've got to get away,' he hissed urgently to her. 'I've got to get away – before it's too late – before I'm not me any more. Don't you see? But how could you? You can't understand – no one can—'

Her nearness was overwhelming – he couldn't bear to be by her another moment. He pushed her away, harder than he meant, so that she fell onto the ground.

'See?' he shouted at her. 'See – it's started already!'

He couldn't catch his breath. He stared at her, sprawled out like that. He was alone and she was different – other

– practically an animal – and that was what he was going to turn into too –

He covered his mouth with his hand and staggered for the door.

Cait: Skara Brae

He'd looked at her as if she disgusted him, like something that had crawled out from under a rock. As if *she* were a ghoul.

Everything was a mess. The house. Rab. Her. *Everything*.

She couldn't bear to think what would have happened if the Old Woman hadn't appeared when she did. Would she really have killed him? But she'd thought that he was . . . that he had . . .

And now he was off, who knew where, and in a terrible state and it was all her fault.

Again.

She scrambled to her feet and followed.

Rab: East of Skara Brae

Outside the door there was a low stone passageway, like a tunnel. Rab stumbled, bent double, along it and then turned to the left, towards the light, erupting from the end of the tunnel into a paved area. The brightness of the sun dazzled him. Through squinting eyes he saw faces, too many faces – horrible and dirty and scarred – they were staring at him – he was assaulted by a whole new barrage of smells – there were animal skins lying about and piles of dead bushes and half-disembowelled fish –

He turned abruptly and saw the village for the first time – weird half-buried lumps covered in scrubby thatch with blue-grey smoke sieving up from each one, twining together and drifting away. Just at that moment, someone propped open a roof window and more smoke belched out.

'Selkie? Can we help you, selkie?'

He spun round. A stunted woman reached out for him and he realised she had only one eye and nothing but a ghastly puckered red pit where the other eye should be.

He flinched away from her in horror but there were more of them, moving towards him.

'Selkie?' It was like a hiss.

Fending them off, whimpering in fear, he staggered away, tripping over stone containers, toppling heaps of vegetation. Past a stone-lined pool of water, his feet found a track that led away from the village. He started to run. He wasn't running towards anything because the only thing he wanted wasn't within reach of his feet. He was running *away*. He had no sense of anything else, just stumbling forward, just putting one foot in front of the other as fast as he could manage. He didn't notice Cait, loping easily behind him, keeping him in view.

He came to the top of a rise and stopped short, unable to understand what he saw. There was nothing there. Nothing at all. No houses, no buildings, no tower stacks, no figures in the landscape, nothing but dead-looking bushes and patches of black mud and scattered pools of water reflecting the sky.

Empty. Utterly, impossibly empty.

He had never seen emptiness before. In his time, there was no such thing. Every centimetre of the world was filled to overflowing. He knew it wasn't like that here, now – he knew it with his mind, from his studies, but his eyes were struggling and his imagination denied their evidence.

'Where are they?' he panted. 'Where are the people?'

Nothing but space – space without anyone to live in it – wasted space – wasted land – wasteland – There was a roaring in his ears and he felt as if he were about to fall – it was as if the ground were juddering –

His knees crumpled. Cait ran up behind him, trying to catch him, but she wasn't quick enough, and instead she only succeeded in tripping herself and knocking him over the edge of the hillock. They landed in a tangle on the springy heather. Rab held onto her as if she were the only thing left in the world, as if he would become nothing himself if he let her go. He buried his face in her shoulder and wept bitter tears.

Cait: East of Skara Brae

She let him be. She didn't understand what he'd been saying or why the view upset him so much. But that didn't matter. He was out of place, that was all. Out of his place. She knew how that felt.

They had landed in a hollow below the crest of the hill. It was warm there, lying on the supporting heather, out of the wind, with the sun beating down. She slitted her eyes against the brightness and looked up into the distant blue. A bumble bee burbled drunkenly past between her and the sky, confused, tricked into waking early. It was out of place too, yet the sound was soothing nevertheless. The weight of Rab, quiet now in her arms, was also comforting.

He sighed deeply. She could tell he had fallen asleep, utterly worn out. She tightened her arms a little and sighed too, as a wave of contentment washed over her. Her eyes fell shut and the light of the sun made red shapes on the inside of her lids until she, too, had drifted off.

She slept so deeply that she didn't feel Rab stir, untangle himself from her and stumble away. Only the dropping temperature as the short day neared its end dragged her, shivering, back into consciousness. The contentment was gone, along with the warmth.

Along with the selkie. What did the stories all say? Sooner or later the selkie always finds his skin. Always leaves. Don't give your heart to a selkie if you don't want it broken.

Well, she was safe from that, anyway. Her heart was whole and set on leaving Skara Brae behind, the very first moment she had her mother safe out of the hands of Voy.

The Old Woman stood in her way and his, equally.

She was heart whole. She was certain.

She made her way back to the village with its familiar smoke and smells. When she ducked under the low lintel and into the Old Woman's house she almost tripped over Rab. He was in a huddled heap just inside the doorway.

He didn't look up. He'd made no attempt to feed the fire or tidy the mess of heather bedding and blood-stained scraps of bog cotton strewn about on the ground.

She got on with sweeping up the debris, remaking Voy's bed, putting everything back in order.

He didn't move, until they heard the sound of the Old Woman's wheezing breath as she crabbed her way along the passageway. Then he scrambled into the other bed box and dropped the hide canopy down.

A moment later, Voy came in, a cooking pot in the crook of her arm.

'Here,' she grunted. 'Sidne sent this for you and the selkie.'

As if nothing had happened.

'He's tired,' Cait said. 'He's gone to bed.'

As if nothing had happened.

Rab: Skara Brae

The next morning he woke with a headache, a face ache, an aching throat – and a determination hard and clear in his mind like a shiny stone. He was going to confront Voy. He was going to demand his Skin. He was going to make her give it to him and he was going to get away from here before . . .

He suddenly realised that he was alone. He'd already missed her – but it couldn't be by much. The door to the passageway was open and he could almost sense the displacement of air of someone passing out of the house. He scrambled out of the box bed, down the stone tunnel and out into the paved place, looking wildly round, just in time to see Voy disappear behind the swell of land behind the village.

He ran after her.

The landscape was as barren and empty as before, and he had to fight the panic that rose in his throat like sick. But ahead of him, Voy's twisted figure hirpled over the rough ground with remarkable speed. He would lose her if he didn't move.

Ignoring the erratic beating of his heart, Rab pushed forward. By the time he caught up with her they were surrounded by the greying heather and the great empty bowl of sky, and there was a metallic taste in his mouth no matter how often he tried to swallow it away. 'Stop! You've got my Skin. I want it back.'

Voy paused and turned round to look at him, her lips pulled back in that grin of hers that hadn't anything to do with smiling. He hated that grin.

She shook her head. 'No.'

'You've got no right to it. It's not yours. You stole it from me when I was too sick to stop you. Give it back to me. Give it back to me *now*!' He could hear his voice rising in pitch. It made him sound weak. He deliberately spoke lower, squaring his shoulders, trying to look threatening. 'I'm warning you.'

The grin widened and she mimicked his attempted growl. 'You're warning me? Of what? Just what do you imagine yourself doing to me, seal boy?'

He wished she wasn't so horribly good at making him shrivel in on himself. He wished he could be facing her when he had the hot wild blood pounding round his body like some ancient warrior. But he was just ordinary, just himself. He'd barely even experienced pain before he came here and the only violence he knew was the no-consequences violence of the vid and of sim games. Nobody ever got hurt. Nobody ever died. How she would sneer at them, if she knew.

'You want it back?'

'What? Yes!'

'Then earn it.'

He had no idea what she wanted. Maybe she meant information. About the future. But what about the Non-Intervention Contract? His Com had been adamant about that. But his Com wasn't here, and he didn't care any more. If there was a bargain to be struck, he would strike it. Anything to get back home. 'What do you want from me?'

84

The grin widened. 'You're lucky. Selkies are lucky. Share your luck with us.'

His mouth dropped open stupidly. 'I don't know anything about that! I can't make you lucky.'

The Old Woman shrugged. 'If you can't make us lucky, maybe you're not a selkie. And if you're not a selkie, it can't be your skin. Maybe you're just another castaway, like the girl, a foundling that Skara Brae has taken in. That *I* have taken in. Living off us. What are you good for? Luck is all you have to contribute, and you say you have none of that.' She lifted one shoulder and eyed him speculatively. 'Why should we keep you, I wonder. Go away, why don't you? Unless the skin is yours. Unless you *are* a selkie. A shape changer. Maybe even a future changer.'

She began to circle round him, slowly, dripping horror and derision into his mind in equal measures.

'Make me believe you. Make me give you back the silver skin. Or maybe you could just *take* it. Why don't you smash my head in with that stone there? Mash my face into the grey pulp inside my skull, splinter the bones, let the blood spurt up. Strapping lad like you, old woman like me, should be no problem. You could slit my throat with a knife. There's one on the shelf. Gairstay, our Old Chert, made it. It has a fine sharp edge. Do you know where to cut? I could show you. Just here, where the life beats in the neck – that's where you must aim.' She bent her head to the side, displaying her scrawny throat. He could see the pulse throbbing just under her wizened skin. 'And then stand back and wait for all the red blood to drain away. Or a belly stab might suit you better – it is sure and needs no special accuracy. Rip open a body anywhere in the soft parts and it will suppurate and stink, you can count on infection setting in, only a little patience is required before death and the rest of the body can follow suit, stinking and putrefying – we turn to liquid more quickly than you might think. All that solid flesh sloughing off my bones till they're clean and white . . .'

He put his hands over his ears, tried to block her out, but somehow he could still hear her. She went on whispering, suggesting and describing more and more horrible ways Rab could take her life. Her words dripped like poison – they smelled of damp earth and fear and sweat, until he couldn't stand it. It was making him sick. He had to stop that awful voice – he had to shut her up. With a strangled shriek he turned and flung himself at her but suddenly she wasn't there and before he could turn again she had slammed her stick into the backs of his knees so that he crashed hard onto his back. All the air was knocked out of his lungs and before he could draw breath again she stood over him, blocking out the sky while the end of her staff bored agonizingly into his gut.

'You want back your skin, seal boy? Prove it's yours. We can't go on with the world the way it is. We need things to change. Make them change. Share your luck. Start with good weather and a clear Road at the Ring of Stones. Keep the clouds away this cycle, so we can release the spirits of our dead from the stones and send them back to the Source. That shouldn't be a problem for a powerful creature like you. Go on. Impress me. Impress us all.' With a sneer on her face, she eased the pressure on the staff, then removed it altogether. Rab curled in on himself, retching and wretched. By the time he could finally make himself stand again, the Old Woman was nowhere to be seen.

He limped back to the village because there was nothing else to do. Nowhere else to go.

Cait: Skara Brae

The selkie had changed. Cait didn't know what had happened when he'd gone chasing after the Old Woman that day. She couldn't guess what Voy had said to him. But she could see the results. As the unseasonably warm days passed, Rab grew stronger and more healthy in body, but there was something far from well going on inside. The smile still came when he turned to her but it had become brittle and stretched. He asked a lot of questions in an odd way. Fast, as if he were trying to cram as many in as possible before . . . before what?

She'd felt close to him during the long, hard illness, closer still when they'd lain together in the hollow in the heather and he'd cried out his heartache, but now, though he spoke to her constantly, he seemed somehow to be someplace else. Every question seemed to be saying *I'm not like you. You're different. Let's make a list of all the ways you're different . . .*

He jiggled his knee unconsciously whenever he sat down.

He had bad dreams.

Rab: Skara Brae

I should be taking notes! If only I could take notes!

The data for a dozen reports, untold credits, square centimetres of floor space, were all around him and he had no recording system of any kind. No Com, no vid, no voice rec. Only his own precarious memory.

It drove him crazy.

He gathered information anyway. He constantly asked questions. Not because he needed to know how this world worked in order to survive in it. Oh no. He wasn't going to be here long enough to need to do that. It was so, when he got home, he could capitalise on the things he was seeing, hearing, smelling. His friends were going to be so jealous. His mum was going to be so impressed.

This is a dream opportunity. This is going to change my life, when I get home.

When I get home.

Sometimes the urge to grab Cait by the arm and tell her the truth about himself – about the world he really belonged in – would build up to a terrible pressure. He fought the impulse with more questions. He pestered her like a toddler.

What's in that field? Why is the Stone Maker's house separate from the rest? What's that big pile of rubbish behind the village? What do the other houses in the village look like?

She'd stared at him when he asked that. 'All the houses are the same – that's how you know they're *houses*!'

Not so different from home, then, he thought and then pushed the feelings that rose in his chest away.

Data. I'm after data.

He watched Cait in the hut, keeping the fire going, grinding grain on the flat stone quern, cooking food and foul-smelling medicines, boiling seawater to produce salt, hanging strips of meat from the whale bone rafters to cure in the smoke. Outside, he watched the villagers, grubbing in the field, bringing limpets and fish from the shore, dried berries and heather from the moors. He watched them in the paved place, talking, hands busy. Some of them laboured in pairs, twisting rope out of crowberry stems and roots. Others were working pieces of leather, rubbing them with lumps of rock. No one was idle, except him.

He watched, and watched, and tried to remember what he saw.

For when he got home.

At first he had trouble telling the villagers apart – everybody had the same leathery skin and scars and marks – or how old they were. Even the few children were so . . . *battered.* Burn marks and old wounds, all puckered and ugly. They all wore the same clothes – trousers and tunics of some sort of felted wool material, cloaks made of animal skins with the fur left on, leather boots laced to their legs. Necklaces of shells and stones, feathers and bones, strung on leather cords. But gradually he became able to see the difference in quality and grandeur in all these things – the skins of Sketh's cloak, for example, were far finer than the ones Rath's was made from, and Mewie's necklace had a special piece of green jadeite and what Cait called an eye stone.

90

The men wore jewellery as well. When Rab first saw the thing in pride of place on Sketh's necklace he had a moment of horror – it looked just like a wizened human hand – the hand of a skeletal child – he had visions of screaming mothers and baby sacrifice . . . In fact, it was the talon of a golden eagle that the hunter had killed – when Sketh saw him staring at it, he proudly told him the whole story, in detail.

The people of Skara Brae did look a lot like each other, but no one in Skara Brae looked like him. For one thing, everybody was smaller than him. Even as weather-beaten and browned as they were, their skin was several shades lighter than his own. And no one had his short black curls. At home, human colouring and characteristics had been jumbled together for so long that any couple could produce a child of any appearance. Nobody stuck out because everybody looked different.

Here, nobody looked like him. And nobody looked like Cait, either, with her height and her pale hair.

In his tower stack and all the other stacks of his world, people were hugely crowded together – of course they were – but Rab had never worried about illness in his life. Whereas here . . .

Disease could rip through a place like this like a fire. He could just imagine the villagers in the middle of some epidemic, bustling about helping each other, going in and out of each other's homes with food and fuel, making absolutely sure the germs were carried to everyone.

It was terrifying. He looked down at his hands, wondering what microbes were breeding in the grime on his skin and under his nails. All at once his throat felt scratchy and snot began to well up in his nose. He felt cold, and the smoky fire and smelly sleeping rugs couldn't warm him. Only sitting in the sun could do that.

Earn your skin, the Old Woman had said. And, bizarrely, Rab seemed to doing so. Day after day, the sun shone and the sky was blue and benign. Nothing could stop the wind, though. It was a new experience for him. At home, it was possible to go up to the roof of the tower stack, but at that height it would be crazy not to have protective shielding. The force fields let in the light but kept the wind at bay, so that it was always still, up there. But here, it was different. He could always hear the wind, whether in the hut or the passageway or in the open. It was present, and it had bugs in it.

In the paved place, though, he could lean against the outer wall of the village and bask in a little protected sun trap. *Just what the selkie ordered.* The villagers' initial caution lessened as time passed and he showed no signs of wanting to suck anyone's soul or dribble blood. Eyes shut, half-dozing, he listened to their whispered conversations.

'Have you noticed – there hasn't been a storm since our selkie arrived?'

'There's a real warmth to the Sun – I can feel it in my bones, and you know my bones never lie.'

'Did you see Benth? She went right over to him and petted his hair!'

'She *never*! What did he do? Did he realise she's *no* idea what she does any more?'

'I'm no expert – he's got such an odd face – but he just let her do it, and then she wandered off again . . .'

'Maybe he hexed her and she just didn't notice . . .'

He tried to learn some of the things they did, much to

92

the hilarity of all. The children especially liked to sit near him and follow him about, in case he was about to do something funny.

Then, when they got tired of teaching him how to make rope or work hides or play complicated games with whale bone dice, Benth would tell stories. She was incredibly old and sometimes couldn't remember her own name or which house was hers, but she remembered all the stories without effort. She told about the trows who lured the unwary piper inside their green hill and took years of his life away – about the stoor worm whose breath was so foul it killed any who came downwind of it – or about the stones that walked to the shores of lochs once a year to bend down their heads and drink. And Rab would get Cait to explain afterwards about the bits he didn't understand.

But not everybody was happy with Rab's presence.

Ailth, the Young Chert, always seemed to be squatting in the doorway of the Stone Maker's house, banging bits of rock together – and watching him. One afternoon, Rab suddenly decided he'd had enough. He pushed off from the wall and walked over to the young man and stared back.

'I'm Rab.' He knew he was looming. He *wanted* to loom.

'Our good luck charm,' Ailth sneered.

'Not really. What are you making?'

The Young Chert was holding a hunk of rock in his hand and striking grey flakes off it.

'Cait found it,' he said. He held it up. 'For me.'

It looked like a lumpy rock, no different from all the other lumpy rocks, but Ailth was acting like the proud father of a chunk of solid gold. But there was something else going on too. There was an edge to his voice, as if he were making some kind of point.

Rab didn't know what the point was. To cover his ignorance, he picked up one of the flakes and drew it thoughtlessly across his thumb –

'Ow!'

A thread of red welled up. Ailth laughed. 'Sharp as a seal's tooth,' he murmured complacently.

'You could have warned me!'

Ailth shrugged. 'I could have,' he replied. 'If I'd known you were going to be stupid enough to slice your own thumb.' And then there was a sudden, subtle shift in his focus.

Rab didn't notice at first, concentrating instead on a mouth full of sucked thumb. Then he saw that Cait had emerged from the main passageway into the paved place. She put her hands into the small of her back and stretched, as if she'd been cramped into one position for too long. Rab guessed she'd been grinding grain.

Ailth was looking at her. There was something proprietorial in his gaze. Something ever so slightly smug. Cait didn't turn her head, but somehow Rab knew that she knew that she was being looked at.

Rab felt red rush up his face. Ailth and Cait – they were – they must have –

'Want some beer?' Before Rab could answer, Ailth had gone into the Chert's house and returned with a jug. 'It's the good stuff. Gairstay taught me how to brew.'

Rab looked around, but Cait had disappeared again and no one else was paying any attention. 'Um, well, sure, why not? Scut! Is it supposed to smell like that?'

Apparently that was, indeed, how it was supposed to smell. Ailth took a huge slurp and smacked his lips appreciatively. He passed the jug to Rab, who tried not to breathe, took a sip and started to cough. The second sip was not quite as bad. The third sip was almost bearable.

'So,' said Ailth suddenly. 'What do you know about the Tears of the Sun?'

'The what?'

'The Tears of the Sun. Bronze. The new material. Some people think it comes from the Fey – your kind. But I think it's an Offlander invention.'

'Bronze doesn't come from the sea, I know that much.' Rab desperately tried to remember from his lectures the order that metals were discovered – bronze then copper? Gold? No, iron, wasn't it? An Iron Age? He'd known all that for an exam years ago, but as soon as he'd sat the test he'd let it dribble out his ears, to make room for the next set of facts he needed to learn.

'It comes from stone – special stone.' Ailth paused his explanation to drink deeply again, and passed the jug back. 'It takes two kinds – you don't even find them in the same place. There's the ones with bits of green – you grind those up, like grain to make flour, you know? And then you put in the other one and heat it up till it's runny and pour it into a hollow shape – *though*—' here he prodded Rab's shoulder to make sure he was listening properly ' – though I've been doing some experiments.' He nodded sagely and put his finger to his lips. 'Follow me.'

He got up and ducked back into the Maker's house. For some reason, when Rab tried to do the same, he banged into the side of the entrance, hitting his funny bone unpleasantly hard. Rubbing it, he straightened up and peered about. The square central hearth was much bigger than Voy's. And the smells were different too. The Young Chert was obviously following in his elder's footsteps in many ways, including brewing something noxious in a collection of jars in the corner. There were more shelves, stacked with antler tools and stone slivers and lumps of rock. There was a sort of oven with some clay lamps sitting on top.

Ailth evidently could turn his hand to most things.

It made Rab want to tell him all the things in his own time that *he* was good at and Ailth would be rubbish at.

That'd shut him up, he thought.

At the moment, though, Ailth was still talking about bronze, and the more he talked and showed Rab lumps of half-melted ore and stones with flecks of something shiny in them and then talked some more, the more incomprehensible it all became.

Which is strange, thought Rab, as he took another gulp of beer. *How hard can it be?*

And then something else wandered into his mind.

'Ailth, listen. You know the Stone Maker who died – he was called the Old Chert, right? And you were his apprentice. But even though he's not here any more, they still call you *Young* Chert. So what happens when you take on an apprentice? What will they call him?'

Ailth took a deep draught from the jug. 'That would have to be, ah, Baby Chert.'

'B-Baby Chert?' Rab squawked.

Ailth got up and started to hobble about the room, hand on his bent back, his voice high and squeaky like an old man's. 'I've seen more cycles than you've got curly hairs on your curly head, I have, and knapped the finest flint in all the islands with these two . . . where'd it go? . . . I used to have two . . . oh, there it is – with these two hands – what was I saying? I'm Baby Chert, I am, and what are you sniggering at, young fellow – beware the wrath of Baby Chert!'

They were snorting so loudly they didn't hear the scratching at the door post at first.

'Ailth?' some one called.

Rab turned and saw the one-eyed woman – Sidne – crouching outside.

Ailth went out and squatted in front of her. Framed by the entrance, Rab could see their faces close together, and suddenly the similarity between them was striking. Sidne handed Ailth a pot of something, patted his shoulder and went back into the village.

'Hey – that's your mother!' Rab said, hardly slurring at all.

Ailth shrugged. 'Hungry?' Without waiting for an answer he scooped a bowlful out and handed it over. 'She's the best cook in the village.'

This was probably true, but the food on top of the beer was a mistake. Rab's stomach rebelled. Spectacularly. Cait came across the paved place in search of him, just in time to see him staggering out of the Chert's house and round to the side, where he vomited.

Cait gave Ailth a look.

'What? How could I know selkies can't hold their drink?' he protested, all wounded innocence.

'Oh yes. Because of course there's all that beer under the sea.'

'Cait?' quavered Rab. 'I feel awful . . .'

'Oh, come on.' And she went to support the green-faced seal boy.

'Need a hand?' asked Ailth.

'No.'

'Will I see you later?'

Cait shrugged. 'I'm always here.'

The weather stayed fair. The wind blew. Rab's body grew stronger. And time passed.

Voy: North of Skara Brae

Day after day, Voy climbed the path up the north head-land, sat by the cairn and thought. If she turned her head, she could see the village from her vantage point. She could see figures moving about the paved place and the smoke rising through the thatch of the houses. And she could see the part of the village where no one lived any more, where no smoke rose. The part of the village where Voy had been born and grew up.

Her family's house, and the others along that passageway, had been empty and sealed for a long time, since the year the fever came. It swept through the village like a fire through dry heather, and by the time it burned itself out, half of the villagers were dead, including her parents and brothers and sisters.

Young Voy had cried for her family, but she knew the reason for all the death.

'With so many spirits being sent to Her,' she said to Hesta, 'the Sun will grow strong again. That's right, isn't it? That's why they all died. To make the Sun strong, and bring the Greater Days back. They'd be happy to do that. Even the babies, if they could understand, they'd be happy.'

Hesta, drained and thin after all her fruitless efforts to save her people, didn't answer.

But young Voy was sure. Things made sense. Dying made sense. It was what you made life out of.

Things are going to get better, she thought. *I'm going to make them better.*

And old Voy looked back on her young, sure self and let the tears drip down her face and onto her ravaged hands.

Hesta had been the Old Woman before her. She'd taken Voy in after the fever and she'd taught her everything she knew. Voy had soaked it all up like a wad of wool and asked for more. More about medicine and what was inside things and about rituals and the First People and power. More about how things used to be and how they were going to be. More about the Greater Days.

'That's long gone,' Hesta said. 'Nothing but ruins now. And memories, but not so many of those either.'

Young Voy had asked, 'Why are they over? I want to live in Great Days!'

Hesta smiled and shook her head. 'You don't get to choose! The bad times need peopled too, don't they, silly? Besides, I'm not sure I'd be happy in all that bustle and busyness. I can't quite see me screeching orders at a building site all day, can you?'

It was true. If Hesta had been in charge of the building of the Ring of Stones or the strange structures on the Ness that no one now understood, they'd have taken aeons to rise as she listened and chatted and listened some more to every workman's worries and aches and pains. But Voy had no doubts at all. She was sure *she'd* have been happy. She could see it easily – 'That stone there! Higher! Straighter!' Striding about, full of the knowledge everyone else lacked. Full of power.

She'd been sure, too, that there would be new Great Days and she would be part of the return to glory. Hesta would teach her everything she needed to know and then . . .

Voy had never doubted she was Old Woman material, though it took Hesta a little longer to realise it.

'It's a fact I'd been thinking of choosing another girl entirely,' Hesta admitted, 'but it would have been a mistake. Her enthusiasms were elsewhere.'

Voy knew about Luatha. By the time she went to a new village she'd lain with near enough every man in Skara Brae.

'They'll be sad to see her go,' Hesta said. 'But it'll be more peaceful in the long run.'

Voy knew about the way babies were made. She knew about how to stop one growing in a woman's belly, too. What took her some time to understand was why anyone would want to do either. When she suddenly did understand, it hit her hard. She thought she would begin to howl at the moon like a love-sick dog. She watched the men go by with hot eyes and a hectic colour in her face.

'You never do anything by halves, do you,' murmured Hesta and sent Gairstay in to her, closing the door from the outside.

Now Gairstay lay in the cairn, and she was dying little deaths. Skara Brae was diminishing as well. After the fever, as the years passed, their numbers had only risen a very little. The number of babies born and growing to adulthood was small. The houses that had been sealed after the fever stayed that way. Women from other villages were reluctant to make bonds with their men.

Even Hesta hadn't been able to charm many of them to come.

Hesta had been tiny and pretty and loved. Everyone was drawn to her. Voy'd never managed to inspire more than the village's fear, but she'd long ago decided that was enough. There had been no peace for Hesta – day or night, they'd come scratching at her door post, bringing gifts and grumbles in equal measure. Hesta always had time for them, always listened, nodding and making it all better, like a mother kissing a baby who's tumbled over. Voy wondered if it was all that love that drove Hesta into the arms of her visions.

They couldn't reach her there. And then, she was gone altogether. And, wrapping her rage round her like a cloak, Voy had moved to the other bed box, sat on the stone seat at the head of the hearth.

It's you they want, but they can't have you. It's me, or nothing.

It wasn't the same.

But it was what was.

Hesta had tried to teach her to be content with what was – she'd tried and tried. Voy had always fought against that acceptance. She'd always believed that she could make things change.

But now she was running out of time.

Cait: Skara Brae

'Come on!'

It was another fine day – Voy was off at the cairn – the morning's work was done – and Cait had a plan.

'Where are we going?' asked Rab, but she wouldn't say.

She led him along the passageway towards the paved place. *Be empty . . . be empty . . .* she thought. She didn't want any of the children trailing after them today. They liked to follow the selkie about, in case he did something odd.

Be empty!

She was out of luck. As she stuck out her head, she saw practically the entire village there. And, at the centre of the crowd, was Sketh.

Sketh. She spat, in her mind. He was looming over his diminutive wife, Mewie, with his legs straddled and arms folded. He enjoyed bullying her in public.

He wrinkled his big nose. She'd obviously just come from the shore with her gathering bag. 'What's that smell?'

'Limpets,' murmured Mewie, eyes meekly downcast.

'I hate limpets!'

Sketh always talked as if what he was saying was news. Astonishing. A revelation.

Rab poked at her from behind. 'What's the hold-up?' he grumbled. 'I'm getting cramp here.'

'Shhh. Wait!'

103

In the paved place, 'I hate them!' Sketh announced again.

Of course you hate limpets, you backside of a trow. EVERYBODY hates limpets. Even other limpets hate limpets. If you don't want to eat them, go kill us a deer. Go on – give us all some peace!

'I am going hunting!' said Sketh. 'I will slay a mighty stag . . .'

Talk, talk! Go if you're going!

'And I will take my son.'

Cait saw Mot's face light up. His first hunt! She also saw how Mewie flinched. Mot was still young, and he was her only living child. He was a gentle boy. It was hard to believe he was truly Sketh's son, but strange things sometimes happened in families. And he adored his father.

Stranger still, thought Cait.

She felt Rab shifting restlessly behind her. 'All right.' And she dragged him out into the paved place, making way for Sketh and Mot as they headed in to collect spears.

'I'm going on a hunt!' shrilled Mot, bright-eyed, but Mewie, trailing behind, said nothing.

Everyone else was dispersing as well. The excitement was over for now. She could hear Ailth, humming tunelessly in the Stone Maker's house. She recognised the sound – it meant he was deep into something.

'Come on!'

She led Rab away from the village, south along the edge of the dunes. As they walked, she watched him sidelong. She liked that he was tall, like her. She was pleased to see how easily he was moving now. He was getting his strength back. *He walks almost as if he's been doing it*

104

his whole life! She had a sudden, vivid picture of Rab galumphing along on his belly like a proper seal . . .

'What's so funny?' Rab asked.

'Nothing.' But she couldn't stop grinning.

He shrugged and smiled back, and lifted his face up to the sun. It was warm and bright and brought out the strange colours of his hair and skin.

Why shouldn't things get better? Why shouldn't he be the answer?

She took his hand and was surprised, again, at how soft his skin was.

'Come on.'

Rab: South of Skara Brae

They moved inland at an angle, towards the Little Loch.
She kept looking over her shoulder, he wasn't sure why.
He found he really didn't care. It was good just to be with
her.

When Skara Brae was behind the swell of the moorland,
Cait turned towards the south headland. They climbed
the slope to the crest of the hill and then down the other
side, so that the bay was out of sight. Rab looked along
this new stretch of coast. Cliffs dipped down to rocky
shores – streams made slate-coloured shapes through the
heather as the fresh water headed for the sea. The wide
open space of the ocean didn't bother him. It was meant
to be empty.

Cait picked up the pace, leading him down at an abrupt
tangent to a jumble of rocks at the base of the headland.
His legs were beginning to complain, when suddenly she
stopped and scanned all about.

'Now. Quickly.' She ducked between the rocks so fast
he lost her for a moment.

'Hey—!'

'Hurry up!' Her voice echoed oddly.

He followed the sound – and found out why.

Hidden among the rocks was the entrance to a cave.
Low at first, so that he had to duck down to enter, it
opened out inside.

Just like a proper house, he thought, without noticing
that what he meant was *Just like a Skara Brae house.*

The space was filled with light. When he looked up, he saw an opening in the rock face that let in the sun. Through it, there was a panoramic view across the waves and along the coast.

Cait was already hunkered beside a miniature square hearth in the centre of the space, fuel at the ready. She took out her flint and sent sparks flying into a little bundle of dry lichen. When a trickle of smoke appeared, she took the lichen up in her hands and blew into it gently, watching closely to see when it was strong enough. Her face was intent. Contented. It made him feel warm inside his chest.

He looked about. There was a fur rug thrown over a pile of heather for a bed, a sitting stone at the head of the hearth, stone tanks in the white sand floor filled with sea water – Cait had even built herself a sized-down set of shelves with a few wonky pots and flint implements. There was a salt tang in the air and the walls were damp to the touch but it had her written all over it.

The fire was going now and already the space was warming.

He realised she was watching him from behind her pale hair.

'This is my place,' she said, half shy, half belligerent. 'I found it when I was little. I used to come here and stare out to sea, hoping that my people would come back for me. That I'd see them coming. Then, after a while, I just came here to get away.'

'It's great. Amazing. What does Ailth think of it?' The words were out of his mouth before he even realised he'd thought them.

She looked straight at him then.

'He's never been here,' she said and held out her hand. His heart was beating hard. 'I haven't done this before.'
'Don't worry. I have.'

He looked into her eyes and saw that there were tiny golden specks in the blue. He was going to tell her about them, but then she put her mouth on his and he forgot everything else.

Voy: North of Skara Brae

It was almost time to leave for the Ring of Stones. Another cycle, another chance to draw the Road down from the Sun, send the loved dead back to the Source. Make the Sun strong again.

We keep doing the same things, Gairstay, as hard as we possibly can, but we keep getting less and less in return. The world grows darker and colder, and we don't know why or how to make it better.

Did she have an answer in the pouch at her waist? There was nothing she was afraid to do – *except nothing! Except doing nothing in an unending fading away. I'm afraid of that.*

She heaved a sigh. She was weary just climbing up to the cairn. She tried to make her brain work, tried to see the way forward. See what she should do, before her people's decline became irrevocable and they were all forgotten.

And her mind drifted ahead, to the Ring of Hills. To the Maes Howe, built at what huge effort by the people of the Greater Days, now deserted. The great ruin on the Ness, between the salt marsh and the freshwater loch. The flattened village by the Lesser Circle.

At least they left something to wonder about. Who will wonder about us? About me?

Gairstay had never had to worry about that. His work would last forever. Stone lasts forever. Down the generations, long after he was gone, people would hold his work in their hands and marvel.

It had taken Gairstay months of patient work to reveal the shape inside each of the spirit stones. Sanding, chiselling, grinding – no two stones alike. Some were rounded, some angular and spiked, some axe-shaped, some shaped like sea urchins, some shaped like nothing in the world . . .

She'd held them in her hands and felt them warming up from her flesh. It was clear that each was the shape that it must be, and could be no other. But . . . 'How did you know? How did you know *this* was inside?'

He'd just smiled. But where Gairstay's skills found the shape inside the stone and freed it, the new material – the one they called the Tears of the Sun – started from an empty shape – a mould, they called it – that the liquid bronze was poured into. Or so he told her. She wondered in passing how he knew so much about it, but then decided it would be the sort of thing the Cherts talked about together when they met at the Ring.

She asked, 'So it's the one who makes the mould who decides what the final shape is going to be?' It was the opposite to what the Stone Makers did in finding what was already there.

It didn't seem right.

She couldn't remember now what he'd said to that. She was starting to lose things in the blank places. Things she knew before she went into one and couldn't find again afterwards. Where did her mind go, in those strange absences?

What if that is the way the world ends? A blankness, then another, then another, until the one from which there was no return.

110

Or would there be children? What if time had children – ages had children –

Who were the children of her time? The ones with the new metal? The Offlanders like the ones that spawned Cait? The selkies?

Gairstay had had a theory.

'I think it's possible the Sun has shifted,' he said. 'I think perhaps some other people have found a new Road that is more acceptable to Her than our old ways. You can't help seeing how much taller and stronger and healthier the Offlanders are. Maybe the Sun's chosen them. Maybe She has gone to shine somewhere else, further to the east perhaps. To where the amber comes from. Or maybe wherever the girl comes from. Or south – the new metal comes from the south. Perhaps where bronze is plentiful the people are using it to draw the life to themselves, so there is less left for us.'

Voy had struggled to picture this. The Sun was the Sun – She moved along the horizon, rising and setting in the same places each year. How could one Sun be in their sky and another Sun be in some other people's sky?

'There is only one Sun.'

'The world is wide,' said Gairstay, 'and the Sun is high.' He drew her pictures in the sand, with lines drawn to show angles and slants and places that the Road might be cut into and weakened . . . Her mind wandered. She didn't think his lines in the sand were the answer, though they seemed to give him satisfaction. Not knowing – that was the thing that rankled. Not knowing, but still being sure that if only she *did* know, she could fix everything. She could do it, if only she knew what it was.

She missed him so much, it hurt like a cracked rib, with every breath.

When she saw the girl at the other side of the bay, leading the selkie over the brow of the hill, her smile twisted, but she let them be.

Cait: South of Skara Brae

Wailing woke them.

Seals, wailing. It was always an unsettling sound, even in bright sunshine like today. The cries faded and rose, drifting to them on the wind – eerie, alien, infinitely sad.

'Is it for you?' she asked Rab in a whisper. 'Are they calling for you?'

'What?'

She knew where they would be. They liked to haul out, fifty, sixty at a time. The tide was low now, and the skerry of flat rocks would be nicely out of the water. Perfect for basking.

'Come on.'

She lead the way out between the rocks and down to the shoreline. They couldn't see the skerry from here, but she knew how to draw the seals' attention. She pulled a whistle bone out of her bag and put it to her lips. The sound was shrill and high-pitched, and almost at once, wet grey heads began to pop up in the waves. Long-nosed faces ending in splendid white whiskers, stiff with curiosity. The tune wailed and wavered. The seals seemed to find it mesmerizing. When she walked along the shore towards the skerry, they followed her, keeping pace like inquisitive, though nervous, aquatic dogs.

On the rocks, other heads lifted and dozens of dark, slightly bulging eyes turned towards them, watching them intently. The wailing stopped, but grunts and sneezes were exchanged. The ones in the water bobbed up higher to get a better view, sank under the waves, then reappeared further along the shore.

Rab smiled. He seemed delighted at the sight, but he made no move to speak to them.

Cait stopped playing. She found she was holding her breath.

Tell them you're all right here on land. Happy and safe.
The words formed in her mind.

Tell them you've decided to stay.

She closed her lips tightly, refusing to say the words out loud, but they pushed at her control so that she wasn't paying attention to anything else. To whatever it was that suddenly caused the seals to lollop into the water in a white, splashing panic.

Rab raised his arms in dismay. 'Oh NO! What—?'

Abruptly she put her hand over his mouth, peering intently along the shore. She heard now what had spooked the seals.

Someone was coming. Fast.

Rab: Beyond the Near Hill

It was Mot, pounding along the narrow trail through the heather as if his life depended on his speed.

Deer, Rab thought. *They were going after deer. What could have gone wrong?*

Mot was white as wool, and sweat and tears mixed and dripped down his face. He was so focused on running that he almost raced past without seeing them.

Cait grabbed him. Made him stop.

'*What's happened?*'

The boy could barely speak. '—oar . . . boar . . . father . . .'

Rab saw a look of fear blossom on her face.

'Where?'

'S-scrubland . . . beyond the near hill . . . he's cornered . . .'

'Not dead?'

'Not yet.' Terror and misery competed in his eyes. 'I only ran . . . away . . . to get help . . .'

Cait shook him fiercely and then let go again. 'That's right,' she said. 'Now *keep* running. Bring the men from the village. Tell the Old Woman.' And when he still just stood, trembling, his thin chest heaving, she gave him a shove that nearly knocked him over. 'GO!'

Rab stared after the boy as he rushed away in the direction of the village.

When he turned to speak to Cait she was gone too, already running in the opposite direction.

*

They hid downwind in the scrubby gorse bushes at the side of the clearing and tried to control their panting. They could see Sketh. One leg was a bloody mess. He had his spear butt dug into the ground, the flint point angled outwards. He had backed himself against a jumble of rocks – he'd probably been trying to climb them to get out of reach when he ran out of time. He was trapped.

Between them, and him, was the boar.

Rab struggled to believe what his eyes were telling him.

The boar was huge. As it paced back and forth, he could see spittle and blood splashed over the coarse bristles on its great chest. Grotesque tusks curved out from its jaws, stained and dripping red.

It must be two hundred kilos . . . and then he peered over his shoulder suddenly, fearfully . . .

'Is it alone?' he whispered.

Cait stared straight ahead. 'Maybe. Maybe not. It's mating season – he'll have been out looking for females. Other males to fight with. You can see he's all sexed up.'

'Oh.' Rab tried to whisper the word, but nothing came out.

'When they charge, they lower their heads and then slash upwards. That's what it's done to Sketh's thigh. See? It's ripped through to the bone. He'll bleed to death.'

How can she sound so calm? But then she looked at him and there was desperation in her eyes and her pupils were huge and black.

Sketh was bleeding hard. His face was pasty and Rab could see a sheen of sweat on his skin. *As long as he keeps the spear up the boar can't get close enough to finish him off. As long as* . . .

116

Sketh's eyes started to roll back in his head and the spear dipped. The boar snorted and stamped a foot forward eagerly, but at the sound Sketh struggled with himself, clawing back consciousness by raw force of will. He re-focused his gaze and steadied his weapon.

It was a heroic effort but it came at a price. The blood oozed out of his wound faster and redder. Rab couldn't believe how much of it there was. It was pooling on the ground and still it came.

'Where are the others? Why aren't they here yet?'

Cait shook her head. 'Too soon. Too far.'

Sketh's life was draining away – he was dying in front of their eyes. *This can't be happening . . . This can't be real . . .*

He was deeply conscious of her, close to him. His mind started to race while everything around him slowed.

He didn't have a spear. He didn't even have a knife. All he had was what was inside his head.

The zoo . . .

Out of nowhere, he remembered going with his friends to a zoo – of course all the species were miniaturized to save space, nothing like the size of the thing in the clearing, but otherwise . . . He'd only been a kid but he'd learned stuff.

Rab closed his eyes, squeezed them tight to block out the terror, focusing on remembering.

Boars are just big pigs. And pigs are smart. That means they have expectations. That means they can be surprised. Distracted. Confused.

The element of surprise. That was what he had. And there was a plan, sitting in his brain, waiting to see what

117

he would do with it. Not a great plan – not even a good plan – but . . .

Rab opened his eyes and stood up.

He heard Cait gasp. He felt her hand on his sleeve. He ignored it and stepped out of the bushes and into the clearing.

'Hey. Pig.'

The boar swung round with terrifying speed. It squinted its short-sighted little eyes. Its nostrils flared red, but the wind was still blowing towards Rab, carrying his scent away. He got a powerful blast of the boar though, a hot, acrid stench that made him want to gag. But there was no time. He had just a split second before the boar made up its piggy mind about what to do with this unexpected, half-sensed new arrival.

'Want to see a dance?'

And Rab began to do his wild, gangly, ungainly victory dance, even though he had no guarantee of victory of any sort. There was no sound track, no music in his head – just the pounding of his heart as he hopped up and down and side to side, arms flailing.

'Look at me. Look at me. Don't look at him. Look at me,' he chanted. His voice was high and squeaky and didn't sound like it belonged to him at all.

The boar snorted and shifted uneasily on its sharp feet. It lowered its head –

Bad sign! Bad sign! Rab added great awkward leaps from one side of the clearing to the other.

The boar gave a bewildered grunt and swung its head back and forth, trying to keep track of Rab's apparently random motion. But confusion was fast turning into irritation. The dance had won the wounded hunter

118

moments, but no more. Rab was already starting to gasp, his muscles beginning to cramp up. The boar seemed to sense weakness. Spittle drooled down from its jaws – again the great head began to lower, preparing to charge, the blood-stained tusks glinting . . .

'Look at me, you big bully – this is what I think of *you*!'

Rab was so shocked he almost stopped moving – but there was Cait, leaping out of the bushes, wagging her bottom and thrashing her arms about and pulling grotesque faces.

Rab could practically see the boar thinking, *NOW what?*

Which is the moment the wind shifted.

Instead of blowing towards them, masking them from the boar, the wind was now sending all the information it needed about these bewildering shapes directly to its sensitive snout. *Is that all?* Another deep sniff. *Is that ALL?!*

With a snort of utter disdain, the boar turned its back on Rab and Cait and prepared to finish its original kill. It took one step.

It never took another.

Spears thwacked into the huge body from all sides. The clearing was suddenly full of men. The boar heaved its great head back and forth, roaring in pain and fury, desperate to focus on a target, but its tormentors were always somewhere else and it was pierced again and again. Rab felt every blow almost as if they were entering his own body. The smell of blood, of dung, of entrails, was shocking, savage.

The boar took forever to die. It lay on its side kicking

and snarling, slashing at nothing, blood and froth spilling onto the ground. When someone finally finished the job, Rab felt his knees go wobbly under him. He crumpled in a heap at the edge of the clearing and was noisily sick.

Cait: Beyond the Near Hill

The second she knew the boar wasn't getting up again, Cait pushed past the mess to get to Sketh. She slid to her knees in the blood-slicked grass.

The hunter's face was a rictus. It wasn't clear if he knew what had happened. He was still holding the spear, his grip so tight she couldn't get it away from him.

'Sketh! Sketh! You've got to let me help you!'

Suddenly someone was beside her.

'Give me the spear, Sketh.' It was Mewie. There was an authority in her voice that made Cait turn her head and stare.

Sketh's hand loosened.

'Now lie down . . .' But even as she was saying the words, the hunter had already collapsed in on himself. As if, without his spear, he didn't remember what his will had been telling him to do any more.

Cait eased him onto his back. When she straightened his wounded leg he whimpered but didn't resist.

White bone showed through the torn muscles and skin. Cait felt sweat break out on her hands.

'Where's Voy?' she called over her shoulder.

'She wasn't there . . . in the village . . .' It was Mot, his sides heaving hugely in and out. Cait wondered numbly just how far the boy had run that day. 'But I brought . . . I went into your place and brought the healing bag . . . I . . .' He swallowed hard and his eyes were afraid. 'I didn't look at anything – I didn't touch anything – please don't punish me!'

Cait surprised herself by suddenly hugging the boy fiercely. 'No one is going to punish you,' she said to him in a husky voice. 'You've done the right thing from first to last and anyone who says otherwise will . . . will . . . live to regret it!' She held onto the hug too long. Anything to keep from facing the ruined thigh.

Inside her head the words kept repeating: *Where's Voy? Where's Voy?*

'I brought water,' said Mewie. Cait reluctantly released the boy and saw the pot of clean water, stoppered with a scrap of leather, tied with crowberry rope. Mewie's terror and doubt when Mot's cry roused the village could not have been greater than Cait's own, now, and yet she'd had the foresight to snatch up the pot. She'd thought through the fear.

For a long moment Cait looked into the other woman's eyes as if she didn't recognise her.

'Tell me what to do,' Mewie said.

'Yes. Wait – I need to . . .'

She needed to look and she needed to *see*. She tried to clean away the blood but it kept oozing up again, blurring what she could see of the gash. She tried again. How could there *be* so much blood?

Voy had had her practising on deer carcasses, cutting the flesh and repairing the wound, again and again. She knew how to work with meat. But without a beating heart to push the blood about there had been nothing like this to deal with. Nothing to get in the way, confusing her.

While she havered, Sketh's life was draining away. He

was already grey about the lips and as she looked at his face she realised he was no longer conscious.

'Tell me what to do,' Mewie repeated.

'Yes . . . yes . . . put your hands here.'

She took Mewie's hands and put them one on top of the other at the place where Sketh's leg met his body. 'There . . . press down. No, harder. That's better . . .'

The blood stayed away for longer now, each time she dabbed it with the puffball. She hoped it wasn't because Sketh was finally running out of it.

She took a deep, slow breath. She closed her eyes and tried to imagine the damage in the dark place inside her head – she could see more clearly there – the way the muscles and tendons and skin should be, and the way they were after the tusk had ripped them apart from each other. What she needed to do to bring them together again, a layer at a time.

You've done this before. A man's no different to a deer. Not much different.

She opened her eyes and reached for the healing bag.

She could see that the tusk had missed the main road of the blood so there was hope for his life, but she knew Sketh wouldn't thank her if she saved his life but he lost the best use of his leg.

She began to clean the wound with the water Mewie had brought and the inner fibres of the puffball fungus – that would slow the bleeding and discourage infection. She drew the long muscles back to their normal places. To what she thought were their normal places. It would be down to Sketh's own strength to knit them together again. Then she took another deep breath and brought out a length of deer tendon.

123

'Mot. I need your hands too.'

She showed him how to hold the sides of the wound together, and she began to sew. She was sweating and her hands cramped with the effort of pushing the sharp bone needles through skin and flesh. But at last it was done. She packed more puffball down along the length of the closed gash and wrapped Sketh's leg from groin to below the knee in felted wool, tying it round with gut straps to keep it straight.

She eased back onto her heels, found she was shaking. She watched as Mewie stroked the hair back from Sketh's forehead. She saw how Mot clung to his father's hand. Something shifted, clenching inside her chest.

Rab: Beyond the Near Hill

The villagers got on with hacking apart the boar while Cait worked to sew Sketh back together again. Both processes seemed to involve appalling amounts of blood.

Scut. It worked. Scut. It worked. That was all he could think as a wave of dizziness swept up from the cold ground.

'Put your head between your knees,' said one of the men, pushing Rab's head down for him with a blood-sticky hand.

That helped. He left it there.

He could hear them whispering. A few words came through – 'Selkie . . . dance . . . dance . . . entranced . . .'

No. No, no, no. They must have seen me – they must have seen me making an arse of myself . . . they must think I've gone like Benth . . .

But he didn't hear anyone snickering. He looked up. He looked over.

They were clustered at the edge of the clearing, as if to leave a space between themselves and him, but somehow, in a way he couldn't quite put a finger on, the space was a respectful one. When one of the men caught his eye he even raised a hand to his brow in a kind of half-salute.

They think I was doing magic. They think that I knew what I was doing. That it wasn't just a crazy gamble. That I wasn't just trying to impress Cait . . .

She knew – and it didn't matter. Suddenly he just wanted to be close to her. He dragged himself upright and skirted the boar butchering. Cait had just stood up too. She turned from the wounded hunter and took a few steps, randomly, as if she didn't know where to go. Her clothes were blood-soaked and there were red smears right up into her hair and her hands were stained with gore and he didn't care.

Voy: Beyond the Near Hill

The Old Woman came from out of nowhere and stood at the edge of the crowd of villagers. She did not choose that they notice her presence, and so they didn't. She listened to their murmurs of awe. She watched as Cait struggled with fear, calmed herself, looked, cleaned, stitched. She saw the Young Chert watching as well. She saw Cait sag into the selkie's embrace. She saw the look on Ailth's face flicker and twist as he turned away.

But when Cait looked round, suddenly aware of something, the Old Woman was gone.

Cait: Skara Brae

She woke in a sweat, disconcerted to find she was in her own bed – except that she wasn't. She was in Mewie's bed. Mewie had insisted. She had insisted on a lot of things, and Cait had been too weary to argue.

Sketh was snoring unrhythmically in the other bed box, and Mewie and Mot were curled up together by the hearth. The fire had been banked for the night. But which night? She put a hand up to the bruised place on her cheek. It was healing. It didn't hurt too much when she pressed it. So, a few nights anyway, since they'd brought Sketh back to Skara Brae.

Getting Sketh home without re-opening his wound hadn't been easy. The men entrusted with carrying him, stretched out on his cloak, didn't need Cait's urging to know how important it was to keep their burden level and unjolted. By the time Skara Brae came into view, their faces were running with sweat. Sketh was sweating too, and his skin was grey, but only a little blood had reddened the dressing.

Behind the stretcher-bearers came the rest of the village. Everyone was laden down with boar meat and bones wrapped in its skin, pots of entrails, the great head, its dead staring eyes still open, still furious – and everyone was exclaiming and twittering like a flock of over-excited sparrows.

Then, as they came into the paved place, there was

Voy. Just standing, leaning heavily on her staff. Looking at them.

The cheerful voices died away – and then swelled up again as everyone suddenly began talking at once, vying to tell her what had been happening, pointing at Sketh, pointing at the bundles oozing boar blood onto the stones of the paved place, gesticulating, acting out the scene in the clearing, praising the now furiously blushing Rab, including Cait in the acclaim.

And Voy had let them talk. She stood, motionless, her face without expression, until all the words and gestures were done.

'It's true, then,' she said to Cait.

Cait misunderstood. For once, she didn't pick up the warning signs. She thought it was about Sketh. She started to detail the treatment she'd given him – cleansing, layering, sewing – when, abruptly, the Old Woman jerked stiffly forward, swinging her staff up and then down. Cait had just enough time to flinch away to the side, so that instead of crashing down on the crown of her head, the wood only glanced off her cheek.

'You put the selkie in danger.' Spittle flew from the Old Woman's mouth. 'I told you he mustn't die – and you took him and you put him in front of a sex-crazed boar.'

Voy raised her stick for another blow. The villagers shifted uneasily, but Cait knew no one was about to come between the Old Woman and the object of her anger.

'*You're* crazy.'

Cait and Voy froze. Everyone gasped.

It was Rab. 'Nobody put me anywhere. We were trying to save Sketh's life! And we did. Though it was mostly Cait.'

Had there been a murmur of approval from the others? It seemed a bit dream-like now.

Then 'I really think we should get him inside, er, don't you?' Rab had said and, amazingly, the villagers had scuttled to obey him, careful not to catch their Old Woman's eye.

Then there was only Cait and Voy left in the paved place.

'If he dies, it's your fault,' said Voy.

It didn't occur to Cait until later to wonder which *he* she meant.

She'd been lucky. Sketh's wound hadn't gone bad. He didn't die. He was strong. For some reason, Mewie was grateful. So grateful she took her own necklace from around her neck and insisted Cait have it. It was far finer than anything she'd ever owned before.

It was an unaccustomed weight round her neck.

All at once she felt suffocated, surrounded by the sleeping village.

I need some air. I need to see the sky.

She slipped out of Sketh's house and crept along the passageway, touching the carved places on the walls without thinking. She expected to have to pull back the bar that closed the main village door at night. But it was already drawn aside.

She paused for a moment, bent double at the threshold. It was Sketh's task, of course, to make the village secure each night and while he had been laid up, Mot had taken on his father's duty. The boy was so earnest, so proud of the responsibility – it was inconceivable that he could have forgotten.

There must be someone else from Skara Brae feeling restless tonight . . .

130

Cait slipped out into the paved place and straightened. She caught her breath at the sudden cold. The selkie's kind autumn was gone. When she looked up at the sky, she could see from the clouds across the moon that the wind was from the sea, and quickening. Abruptly the full whiteness of the moon emerged in the black sky.

She ducked her head, hurriedly closing her eyes, but her night vision was gone. She waited, silently sniffing the cold air, listening for any sign of who might be out there. The hairs on her arms and the back of her neck tingled – and suddenly she knew.

She opened her eyes and there was Voy, standing at the far edge of the paved place. She was looking inland.

The Old Woman spoke without turning her head. 'It's time. We leave tomorrow. Choose someone to stay with Sketh.' She was holding the selkie's skin in her hands. Cait caught a shimmer of silver, and then the clouds dimmed the moon's light again. When it re-emerged, the skin was no longer in sight. Voy had returned it to the bag at her waist. But it was still there, in the night, with them. A powerful presence. Powerful . . .

Poor Rab! My poor selkie! Would Voy ever let either of them go? And then a tiny voice at the back of her mind whispered, *But if Rab stays, how bad would it be if I stayed too . . .?*

She was so full of her thoughts that she hardly noticed as the Old Woman stumped past on her way back into Skara Brae. And then, unexpectedly, she thought she felt something on her bruised cheek, feather light, almost like a gentle touch.

But when she spun round, there was no one there.

PART THREE

Rab: The Way to the Ring of Hills

Old Benth was to stay behind to tend Sketh but everyone else in the village, from the youngest to the oldest, was up and ready to leave at first light. The adults were laden down with carrying bags and baskets full of food, sleeping hides and fleeces, skins for lean-tos, cooking pots, fuel. The children were doing their best to look appropriately solemn and, for the most part, being much too excited to succeed.

Rab kept trying to get near to Cait. Ever since the day of the visit to the cave he'd thought of little else. He wished he was brave enough to take her hand, right there, with everybody watching. But since they'd brought the wounded hunter back to the village, he'd barely seen her. She'd been busy keeping Sketh alive, of course. But was it just that? She seemed . . . distant. Hugged inside herself. She was watching Voy – well, she was always watching Voy but there was a new wariness in her face, as if she weren't quite sure what was going to happen next.

But that was ridiculous. She'd been to the Ring of Stones every cycle of her life. Why should it be different this time?

When we get back from all this fuss, we'll talk properly. There'll be time then. The thought cheered him up. *She hasn't changed. She's just preoccupied.*

The weather *had* changed though. Rab couldn't stop shivering. Even now the sun was fully up in the sky, frost still showed in the hollows of the hills and in the shadows of rocks.

The track led inland, away from the village, away from the sea. The emptiness of the landscape still made him a bit queasy but at least, he told himself, he'd got better at hiding the way it made him feel.

Or not.

Mewie was suddenly at his elbow.

'Don't worry, selkie,' she whispered, peering up at him. 'The sea will be near again when we get to the Ring of Hills.' Then her voice took on the singsong tones of something learned by rote. *The place of the sun and the moon, the salt and the fresh, the water and the land, the stones and the sky. The place where the roads meet.* See? It'll be all right.'

She patted his sleeve encouragingly, then dropped back to chivvy Mot.

Rab blushed, feeling like a fraud.

There seemed no particular order to the column of travellers. People moved along the track or to either side or surged ahead or stepped aside for others. When he spotted Cait, she was already well ahead of him, near the front. She was moving easily. Powerfully. Gracefully. He found himself staring at the way her hips moved, the way her clothes slid over her backside and thighs. It was mesmerizing . . .

Tripping over a roughness in the path at this moment brought him back to himself with a jolt.

'Steady, seal boy,' growled Ailth who had come up behind him unnoticed. The expression on his face made it clear he knew *exactly* what Rab had been thinking about. *Scut! Is everybody a mind-reader now?* This time the blush that raced up Rab's neck stayed there for a long while.

The emptiness of the moorland continued to unsettle him. As they came over the rim of each hill, he kept looking for signs of people or habitation, but each time there was nothing. Just brittle winter heather, russet bracken, flashes of open water fringed by the last white rags of bog cotton. There was a mournful scream in the huge sky, answered by another – a pair of buzzards circling on invisible thermals, watching for prey.

How small we must look from above. Ants scuttling across the world on ant business . . .

He took a ragged breath and walked on.

After several hours of tramping they came to a place where another track, snaking down from the north, joined theirs.

Rab sidled up to Cait. 'So that's the track the northern villages come in on?' he asked, pointing. He said it for something to say.

But, surprisingly, Cait shook her head. 'That's the track *all* the villages come in on. The ones from the east and south as well.'

'But why? Isn't there a track from the south?'

'Of course there is. It joins this one over the next rise.'

'So why don't the villages from down that way use it?'

'They do! On the way home. All the villages except ours go home that way.'

'I don't understand . . .'

She made an impatient noise. '*Think* about it! The Ring of Hills is what?'

'I don't know – a ring? A circle?'

And then he remembered. She'd explained to him about walking round circles and deosil and widdershins.

'There's only one entrance into the Ring of Hills. It's closest to us. Everybody else has to come round the Ring. Deosil. Sunwise. It's obvious.'

Obvious. So some of these people, who will have been on the road for several days maybe already, get to add another day's walking in a great big pointless circle.

But at least he'd got her to talk to him.

Back off now, though. He kept away from her for the next while, until the track brought them to the brow of a final rise. A lush, low valley lay ahead, the circling hills rising like the sides of a great bowl. The bracken glowed amber. He saw a herd of deer flow up and over the hill opposite. Not so very long ago, he wouldn't have spotted them, or noticed that the grass here seemed greener and taller than the pasturing round Skara Brae. Or, where the soil showed, that it seemed so much richer and darker than the used-up dirt of the Skara Brae fields. But he noticed now.

Whoever lives here is lucky! he thought, looking about for the domed roofs and rising smoke of a village.

There was smoke, but no houses. Instead, there was an open-air gathering of many people, with campfires already started and bed places laid out by the shores of an inland loch. *That must be the fresh water.* From the west, another loch shape fingered into the valley, but it was marshland – salt marsh? A cloud of shore birds flew up from the reeds and then settled again.

'Fresh and salt,' he muttered, trying to remember. 'Sun and the moon, wet and dry, up and down.'

'The stones and the sky.' It was Cait. She was standing beside him, close to his shoulder, looking out over the valley. He was aware of her body in a way that made him

138

want to shout out loud. He felt the blush coming up his neck again and forced himself to focus on the view.

'Yeah. Right. Stones and sky,' he repeated her words, not really taking in what was in the distance.

'There!' She nudged his shoulder and pointed. He looked where she indicated – and there it was.

The Ring of Stones.

A circle of thin megaliths, more than he could count, rising out of the russet of bracken and the green-grey mounds of heather, reaching up into the dying light of the sky. They were surrounded by a bank and a water-filled moat. In the centre there was a raised mound, with a dark smudge at the centre of that.

An early owl cried, disturbed by the strangers in its territory. Its voice was pale and piercing.

As Rab stared out across the valley he started to see other structures, wrecked and half-buried in the ground. A jumble of stone walls and ruined buildings stuck up confusingly in swathes of heather and gorse, spreading across the boggy-looking land bridge that divided the loch from the salt marsh. *What is all that? Some sort of temple? A town?*

And beyond that . . .

'Look, there's another one!'

A smaller circle of standing stones with moat and banks. *And that looks like a village – what's left of a village – over by the loch*. He turned his head to ask Cait about that when his eye was caught by another glint of slant afternoon sunlight on water, even further away. He squinted, not sure what he was seeing, but then he realised it was a mound – a great green mound – like an enormous house, but with a moat around it and a bank around that, like the moats and banks round the two stone circles. And between that place and the place where he stood there were scattered, individual megaliths. Leading down to the encampment, and from the encampment to the larger ring, he could see there were well-defined pathways, but everything else in the valley was covered in unbroken heather and grass. It was clear that part of the great Ring of Hills had been deserted for a long time.

Deserted, in plain sight. Rab noticed that whenever the villagers accidentally found themselves looking in the direction of the mound or the smaller circle, their eyes slid aside and they turned away.

The polite thing to do would be pretend I haven't seen them either, Rab thought to himself. *Too bad.*

'What's that?' he asked, pointing.

'That is the Maes Howe,' Cait said in her singsong I-know-this-from-memory voice. 'It is a place from the Greater Days. Long ago, the people who came before us knew many secrets, about this life and the next life and the ways between them. They were the ones who built the great circles and raised the watch stones – and the Howe. Every cycle, they would cross over the bank and the moat and take away the stone from the doorway. They went into the heart of the Howe and the Sun followed them, revealing mysteries.'

'And then? What happened to them?'

'No one knows for certain. It is thought that a sickness came, and between one year and the next so many of them died that the few that were left forgot everything except scrabbling to find enough food to stay alive. By the time their numbers had grown again, enough to care

140

for their fields and flocks and not be facing starvation every winter, it was too late. The knowledge of the Howe was gone.'

'What's inside it?' Rab asked, lowering his voice, and again Cait replied, 'No one knows for certain. It is said that the Howe is filled with the bones of the great Healers and Hunters and Cherts. It was the highest honour their people could pay them, to lay them in such a tomb.'

'And what happened to the ones who built the other things – the other circle, and the ones who lived in that village and the ones who made that mess of walls in between?'

'That was in the Greater Days.'

'Yes, but you must know *something*!'

Cait didn't answer. She just shook her head and looked away.

The Greater Days. Suddenly they were more than just words. He stared out across the valley – a valley full of history they didn't understand and were afraid to even wonder about.

'Voy says we are a pale people compared to them,' said Cait.

This time Rab took her cold, rough hand and held it tight and, just for a moment, she let him.

Voy: The Ring of Hills

Voy stared out over the great bowl of the valley, listening to the girl's garbled explanation. Had she taught her so poorly? Or did she just not care? That was how it was lost, the knowledge of things. Like the carvings on her bed edge or the cryptic scratches in the long passageway. Oh, the villagers touched them for luck, every time they sidled past, but nobody knew what they meant any more. Times past became times that never happened because some stupid girl was too interested in the fantasies in her head to listen properly. To commit to memory. To be committed to the memory.

She remembered *everything* Hesta told her. Even at the end, when it was all so much babble that came out of her mouth – *I could still quote every word.*

I wonder why I'm thinking about her so much . . .

'Go away and bar the door, Voy,' Hesta would say, and Voy would sigh and do as she was told. She'd squat in the passageway, guarding, waiting, listening to the strange moans and thrashings from within. Worrying. Until a small, wearied voice would call to her, and she would unbar the door and go in.

'What did you see this time?' she used to ask, as she cleaned the room and washed Hesta, rank with strange-smelling sweat and, often, vomit and urine.

Strange tales, the ones Hesta told her then, with the black centres of her eyes tiny points or huge pools, depending on the draft she'd taken. Much of it was senseless, even to Hesta herself, and Voy hoped this might convince her to stop her experiments.

But then all that changed. Hesta had found something new to take.

'I think I must have become a bird, Voy, because I was very high up, looking down on the village and the bay, so high up I could see the Ring of Stones if I turned my head and the Lesser Ring and right to the far shores, north, south, east. But no bird could have hung there so long because I swear I watched for years and years, thousands of years. Where the bay is now, was eaten up by a great white wave – snow and ice that raced down from the north, covering everything, and then as suddenly as it came it was gone again and the bay and the islands were changed into green, steaming forests with animals – such animals, Voy, you wouldn't believe – greater than whales, but with thunderous thick legs, walking through bogs that smoked like a pot on the hearth, and the land was sailing like a cloud overhead except that it was underneath and it was green, a hundred greens . . .'

It was all just another poisoned nightmare, but Hesta was utterly convinced. 'I've seen time! I've seen the life of the world!'

She kept going back for more. 'I have to know.'

'Why?' Voy demanded. 'Why do you have to know? It's past – it's gone – even if it's true, what *good* does it do?' and 'If you have to find out about what came before, why not find out about the ones who built the Maes Howe? The ones who built the Rings? The ruins in the Ring of Hills? Find out what happened to them!'

Hesta just smiled. She had always had such a lovely smile, but her face wasn't pretty any more. Her teeth were coming loose and falling out, and it hurt to eat, so she didn't, much.

'Why don't you see the future, if you have to see anything at all?' Voy grumbled under her breath. 'Find out what's going to happen to the crops this cycle and when Benth's baby's going to come and things that *matter*! Or just fix the Sun while you're about it.' She sounded waspish, even to herself, but she was losing Hesta and she was afraid. Then she could have bitten out her tongue, for Hesta heard her.

'Fix the Sun . . .'

She became obsessed, spending more and more time behind the barred door, leaving the villagers with no one but Voy to tend to them.

'Perhaps more of this and less of the other . . . perhaps boiling less . . . or more . . . in mead . . . in ale . . .' She tried one noxious potion after another, seeking a way into a vision of the future.

'Stop! Stop! I was wrong – the past is what we need to know about! We can't know the future – it doesn't exist, that's why you can't see it.' Voy argued and pleaded and wept, all to no avail.

'Can't you see – if I know what is coming, I will know how to lead the people in the right direction,' Hesta snapped in rare impatience. 'I will know how to make things better. Stop the blight. Make the Sun warm again.' Then she smiled as if to take the sting out of her words. She was all lit up inside. She was so thin that Voy could see the blood pulsing in the veins of her forehead.

And then one day Voy waited outside the barred door and no call came. When she couldn't bear the silence any longer she went in without a summons. Hesta was lying on the floor, limbs sprawled out as if she had been thrashing wildly, blood dried around her mouth and nose. She had stiffened. She had been dead for some time. Eventually the limbs would relax again, but until then there was nothing Voy could do with the contorted body except watch and weep.

Except that the tears wouldn't come. The white rage inside her seemed to dry them up. *You did this to yourself!* she stormed silently, staring down at Hesta with eyes that burned and ached. *You talk to me of contentment with the way things are and then you do this to yourself – to me! How could you be so stupid – how could you be so cruel?*

I will never forgive you.

Back in the here and now, she put her hand on the bag hanging from her waist. And she led her people down the hill.

Cait: The Encampment by the Loch of Harray

'She knows how to make an entrance, that Old Woman.'

'Cutting it fine, aren't they?'

'Shortest distance to travel, last one to arrive . . . just showing off, *I'd* say.'

'You'd think that was one village that wouldn't want to draw attention to itself!'

'Look – they've collected another freak!'

'*Midden!* It's ugly, isn't it?'

'Imagine breeding that with the big pale-haired one – ugh, trows would look pretty beside what would come out of her!'

Cait didn't turn her head, but she knew that they knew that she had heard every word. Rab tried to catch her eye but she just shoved a pot at him and told him to bring some water up from the shore.

They'll be singing another tune when they find out Skara Brae's brought along its very own selkie, she thought. The news would be round every hearth fire before Rab got back from the loch. He wouldn't look so ugly to them then.

Anyway, what does it matter what they think? She ignored the feeling that was like a tight band round her chest and went on helping set up their part of the encampment, round the same square hearth they'd always used, as the afternoon began to fade and the loch turned the colour of slate in the failing light. It only mattered what they might know, this time, what they might have heard since they all gathered here last. Nothing would stop her going about to each hearth, like she always did, asking the same questions she always asked.

Had anyone been visited by strangers? Had any Offlander boats been seen? And – most foolish question of all – had anyone been asking about her? Looking for her? She would ask and they would shake their heads and not bother hiding their scorn.

They would sneer and she would swallow it and go on asking. Her own people – that was what was foremost in her mind. Always. Her own people.

Rab: The Encampment by the Loch of Harray

As the winter day faded, villagers were getting themselves settled around the scattered square hearths cut in the turf. Deerskin lean-tos sheltered the very old and the very young. Rab could smell food cooking over the flames. As he passed, each group fell silent, studiously not looking directly at him.

I'm like the green mound, he thought with a shiver. *I'm like something that shouldn't exist.*

He walked on, clutching the pot, trying to look as if he knew what he was doing. After living with so few people, and in spite of being so uncomfortable with the empty spaces, he was now completely thrown by the number of figures moving round the camp fires.

The sooner this ritual stuff is over and we can get back to Skara Brae, the better.

Ice had formed at the edge of the loch. He hesitated, uncertain how to deal with drawing the water without getting his boots wet. He put a tentative foot onto the ice and hopped back again quickly as it bent and creaked and the water slopped over it.

'Rab! Wait for me!' It was Mot. He ran up and took Rab's hand. It felt cold and clammy. It felt good. 'Cait sent me.'

'She probably thinks I'll get lost or fall in the loch.'

Mot grinned up at him. He grabbed the pot from Rab and used the bottom of it to break the ice, then deftly tilted it on its side and let the water flow in.

When it was full he handed it back to Rab, who pulled a face.

'All right, very clever. I would have figured it out eventually.'

'I'm hungry,' said Mot.

Rab heard the whispers rising up behind him as he followed Mot away from the loch side.

'Is that it? Is that their selkie?'

'What else could it be? Stars, I'd no idea they'd be so ugly! It's the colour of turds!'

'Shut up – hasn't the weather been milder lately? I heard it's turned their luck and no mistake! They've brought boar meat to share!'

'Yeah? I heard Sketh got gored getting it – nearly died. You notice he's not here this time.'

'Yeah, well, I heard he's not dead. Went against a boar the size of a whale AND HE'S NOT DEAD! I'd call that luck.'

'Ignore them,' Mot whispered over his shoulder. 'They're just jealous.'

There were square stone hearths laid into the turf, large communal ones, but Rab noticed that not all of them had people clustered round them. There were almost as many again that were left unlit. Some were hardly visible in the encroaching bracken.

'Why are there so many hearths not being used?' he asked. They seemed sad, all overgrown and lonely with so much bustle and life round the others.

Mot shrugged. 'Because there aren't as many villages as there used to be.'

Rab felt a shiver go down his back and huddled his clothes closer. 'Why? What happened to them?'

Mot shrugged again. 'They died,' he told him. 'Sickness, maybe, or trows.'

'Or maybe they just left?'

The boy looked up at him, his forehead furrowed. 'Where would they go?' he said, and Rab had no answer to that. In his time, people didn't go someplace else because everywhere was already full, but here and now, the world was wide and empty and full of dangers.

'Did anybody go and check?'

'Oh yes. Somebody would always go and check, when a village didn't appear for a cycle. They'd go and watch for a day and a night, from a safe distance. But if there was no smoke, then they'd know.'

'So they're still there ... only they're all dead ...' Pictures pressed their way into Rab's mind – villages just like Skara Brae, only cold and dark, silent except for the wind howling through the passageways and ruffling the clothes of bodies, lying along the ground, women and men and children and babies ... And no one coming close while they were dying and no one coming to collect their spirits when they were dead.

Not that that matters, of course. That's just superstition.
He handed over the pot of water to Mewie and hunkered down by the Skara Brae hearth.

And the cold sick feeling of a stone in his belly? Ignore that too?

It must just be nervousness. That must be it – this was going to be a weird couple of days. He should be excited – this was an amazing opportunity! He was going to see an ancient ritual at first hand – none of the usual trying to make something up out of an inadequate handful of broken artefacts. What had the lecturer said? 'When you

150

really can't figure out what something is, it's easiest to just say it has a ritual purpose. Who's going to be able to contradict you?'

Well, me! thought Rab, just as his emotions veered off again and he found himself desperately pushing down homesickness and the memories of that bright clean world of lectures and cheerful ignorance. He turned to Cait and began to ask, 'What happens n—' when a loud blustery voice bellowed so close behind him, it made him fall off the stone he was sitting on with a yelp.

'Hurry up! Stop all this gossiping and sitting about! Show some respect! Get in line!'

A small man wearing a magnificent cloak of overlapping otter skins was doing a good imitation of looming at them. His forearms were bare and Rab could see the muscles showing like cords. His face was like a discontented sack of walnuts.

'Who's that?' he whispered to Cait, who stuck out her tongue.

'That's Tron of Piggar.'

'Piggar? He's from a place called *Piggar*?!' Rab couldn't help the snort of giggles coming out.

Tron froze for a split second then went back to chivvying the women.

'He wouldn't be pushing everybody about if Sketh were here!' added Cait. Rab wondered if she'd meant to speak quite that loudly.

Tron narrowed his eyes, but didn't seem to know who'd spoken. He pushed Mewie as she hurried past with her arms full of fuel. She stumbled and fell with a squeal, dropping her bundle.

151

Then, suddenly, Voy was there. With a curt nod, Tron moved on.

'Piss-face,' muttered Cait.

'Piss-face from Piggar,' sneered Rab, but the stone in his belly was still there.

Voy: The Encampment by the Loch of Harray

Voy made herself into a still point amongst the bustle and disorder. At this stage, the people around her were all just themselves, just the Living, silly and messy and ordinary. And petty and vindictive and divided and weak and . . . you could go on for hours about the failings of the folk. But there was a change coming. When they would become more than those things – less themselves and more something else –

'Shouldn't we be starting?' the girl asked her, getting restless. But Voy ignored her. She had already decided their place in the procession.

Soon. It's almost time . . .

She sniffed the air. The smell of the wind was sharp and cold and did not bode well for a clear Road. Would Gairstay and the others have to wait again? She had the spirit stone safe in a pouch, hanging from her belt, on her right side. It was a comforting, solid, familiar weight. And on her left side, in another bag, was the selkie's silver skin. It weighed near to nothing and when she took it out it would flow through her bent fingers like water, or mist over a stream that the Sun had warmed.

Voy smiled.

Rab: The Ring of Stones

It began as a jumble, people shoving and hissing at each other, trying to locate over-excited children and then keep them under control, torches being lit, one from another, passing from hand to hand.

Rab started to get impatient. *What a mess – in the vids and the simulations these ancient rituals were made up to be all choreographed and solemn and awe-inspiring, when really it's just a lot of standing around in the cold and people bickering.*

But then, gradually, something shifted. The scrum evolved into a procession. As the path of circles began, lit by dozens of torches flaring in the cold wind, Rab became aware of a feeling of focus, of concentration. It was different from anything he had ever experienced before. The procession circled the ditch, then crossed the causeway and circled again, this time along the inside of the Ring of Stones. How many feet had followed this course over how many years? They had worn down the way into a groove. Circles of torchlight moving, outlining the blackness of the ditch, reflecting off the tall grey faces of the standing stones. He wondered what it would look like from above – *what's the word for that?* For a moment he couldn't remember. *Sky view – no, aerial view. Of course. Tip of my tongue. The aerial view would be amazing.*

He shrugged off the odd memory blip and let the lights fill his eyes. Voy had set Skara Brae at the tail end of the great snaking column, so that the full winding maze and blaze was before him. Around him. He shivered, and not from the cold.

And then he saw that the front of the procession had turned inward, arrowing along the straight way that led from the entrance to the central mound. It circled at the centre and then unfurled into the surrounding space.

At last he and the others from Skara Brae were approaching the centre of the Ring too. He could see the mound and on it a great square stone hearth piled high with the fuel that all the villages had brought. At the north side of the hearth there was a free-standing set of shelves on which had been placed the spirit stones from the different villages. When Voy laid the stone carved by Skara Brae's Old Chert beside the others, he felt a surge of pride at the skill and fineness of the work.

And around the hearth were the offerings. Bowls of food and barley ale – carefully crafted pottery jars and flint blades – skins of animals and the wings of birds. Each village had something fine to offer. To put into the fire to please the Sun. Attract Her attention. Open the Road.

Except he couldn't see anything that *they* had brought! He turned anxiously to Cait and whispered, 'Where's ours? We don't have anything—' but she was staring past him.

Tron of Piggar had stepped up onto the mound.

He was a showman, that was certain. He waited a long moment, to be sure that all eyes were on him, then with a big gesture, he swirled his magnificent otter-skin cloak.

There was a murmur of awe.

155

'It'll have taken his woman months to sew that.'

'A fine offering indeed.'

'If anything can appease the Sun . . .'

What a waste, thought Rab.

But Tron had something else in mind. With another conjuror's gesture, he produced a bundle from under the splendid cloak. He let the wrappings drop to the ground and held the object up suddenly, turning in a slow circle so all could see.

An axe. Fire-coloured, set in a wooden haft. The darkness of the wood was a dramatic contrast to the dull sheen of the metal.

Bronze . . .

A ripple of whispers echoed the word in Rab's head, vibrating from the circle of stones in strange patterns of sound. So near the centre, it seemed to him as if hissing waves were surrounding him, passing over his head and returning like surf on a shore.

'The Tears of the Sun,' announced Tron. 'A substance both precious and rare. Till now, this has only been a rumour. A whisper from the south. But not any longer. As you can see. It comes from fire and I will return it to the flames, and the Road to the Sun will open.'

Ahhhh . . . And the sigh returned, *ahhhh . . .*

'Very nice,' said Voy softly, yet, because of the strange acoustics of the Ring, her voice carried to every person there. *Niiisss* came the echo. 'Pretty.' The echo sounded like *piiittteee*. As she spoke, Voy was untying a bag at her belt. She began to draw something like moonlight out of the leather mouth, gently and without fuss. She walked quietly around the top of the mound. Without appearing to ask for attention, she held the eyes of every person there, as she cradled something in her arms like a precious child.

Rab's breath died in his throat. Skara Brae had something to offer to the Sun after all.

His Silver Skin.

Cait: The Encampment by the Loch of Harray

Every cycle, after everyone had left the Ring of Stones and the entrance was sealed for the night, it was always as if a load had been lifted from the shoulders of the people. Cait noticed it each time, and felt it in herself as well. It was an interval of ordinariness between the first procession and the second, just before daybreak, when they would all return inside the Ring of Stones, light the fire, wait and watch and hope that the offerings would be acceptable. As one again. But for now, there was nothing anyone could do except be themselves.

Conversations broke out, as bright and warming as the cooking fires of the camp that pushed back the night. Babies were shown off and, doubtless, quietly compared in the mothers' minds unfavourably to their own. The old men passed round the barley ale and complained about their bones. Children renewed friendships, raced about, snatched food from whatever pot was nearest and evaded bed time. The young men and women eyed each other speculatively. There were whispers and giggling to be heard off in the privacy of the dark.

Cait was restless. She looked for Ailth around the campfires, but he was deep in animated talk with the Chert from that piss-face Tron's village, and then, before she could attract his attention, he was off whispering to Voy.

Where was Rab?

She found him sitting by Mewie's fire, swaddled up

in sleeping furs so that only his head showed. He was staring into the flames, his face closed off and miserable. He was brooding about his skin.

She hesitated. There was nothing in the stories about anyone ever *destroying* the skin of a selkie. *But what if it works?! What if Voy is right? What if this is the way to heal the Sun?* If that were true, he must see how important that made him. He was their luck. He was their hero. She tried to hide from the thought that, also, without his skin, he would have to stay with her. She felt a need for him suddenly that was more than restlessness. She went over to stand beside him, in the hope that he might look up at her and smile. That she might be able to draw him away from the light for a while.

He didn't seem to notice her at all. Mewie was watching from the other side of the fire. Cait caught her eye and they exchanged wry half-smiles. She shrugged, went round to help Mewie finish a bowl of ale and then, rolled up in her own furs, turned in for the night. Nothing would happen now until the dawn.

It's too cold anyway, she thought to herself and half-way through a yawn that showed white in the air, she fell asleep.

Rab: The Ring of Stones

It had been easy.

As soon as Cait and the others were settled in their sleeping furs, he'd silently slid out from his own. He'd mounded them up to look as if they were still occupied. Then he'd just slipped away.

No one paid any particular attention to him as he passed through the camp and into the darkness beyond. His breath puffed out in nervous wisps. He glanced up and for a moment there was the moon showing over the hills. It was at the full. Then the clouds covered it again. He realised he'd crouched automatically, to be less conspicuous in the sudden light. Part of his mind noticed this with a kind of remote surprise.

He could see where Voy and the other Old Women were camped out by the causeway, guarding the entrance to the Ring. He moved away from them, on across the rough ground, following the curve of the bank and ditch. He kept stumbling and stopping to make sure no one had heard the noise he was making over the chilly soughing of the wind. It would seem that no one did.

The standing stones lurked at the edge of his peripheral vision. He didn't like to look at them directly.

Far enough. He made himself stop. *This is far enough – as good a place as any – you can't just go round the Ring forever.*

The clouds had thinned again so that there was enough light to look down into the ditch. It was filled with water.

He could see there was ice on its surface. Would it hold his weight? *Of course it will, in this cold! Inches thick, at least.* But the thought of breaking through and dropping into the black water held him rigid on the verge. How deep would it be? Over his head? If he fell through would he pass out with the cold and drown and they'd find him the next morning staring up through the ice like a corpse at a window and he'd never get home . . .

You'll never get home standing around peeing yourself either. He pushed the image of his own dead body out of his mind as best he could and slithered down the bank of the ditch. He felt at once how the steep sides blocked the bite of the wind. He teetered for a second on the edge of the ice and then, hunched over, knees bent, he crabbed out cautiously onto the frozen surface. The ice creaked. The sound made sweat break out on his cold face. He swallowed hard – made himself inch forward – 'Hurry up! Hurry up!' he whispered, but nothing on earth could make his feet move quicker – slide, pause, slide, pause, creak, slide, slide . . .

At the last moment he panicked and flung himself forward face first onto the other bank and clung to it with numb fingers, his breath panting into the air in white frantic puffs. He lay there for a long while before he could make the shaking stop, get to his hands and knees and crawl upwards. As he pulled himself up over the lip, the moon slipped out from behind the clouds.

He almost turned around and went back.

161

Cait: The Encampment by the Loch of Harray

She needed to pee again. What was it about cold weather that made you have to bare your bottom so often, getting even colder in the process? She tried to ignore the pressure and go back to sleep, but her bladder was having none of it. She groaned and sat up. She glanced across at the lump of furs that was Rab, curled up on the other side of the fire. He hadn't stirred an inch.

When she came back, shivering, from the latrine ditch, he was still there.

Lucky him, she thought, burrowing into her own nest, hoping to find any of the warmth she'd left behind. *Lucky* . . . and then she was asleep again.

Rab: The Ring of Stones

He crept forward, into silence. Strangely, the night wind that blew outside the Ring did not blow here. The cold bit just as hard, but the air was still. Rab listened and it was as if something listened back. His breath came shallow and fast and hung like mist before his face.

Go back. Go back. The words spoke themselves in his mind.

The stones were black against the bowl of the hills and the sky. Clouds blurred the stars and caged the moon, letting its light out only a little at a time.

You shouldn't be here. You're wrong here.

'It's true,' whispered Rab, clenching his hands. He was wrong here. But without the Silver Skin he couldn't get right. Ever.

He made himself take a step, then another. He made himself walk towards the centre.

He felt like a thief.

'But it's mine,' he whispered, his words white shapes in the air. 'It's mine.'

She'd stolen it from him, when he was hurt and out of his head and couldn't do anything about it. He needed it back and she wouldn't give it to him. Nobody could call this stealing. He wasn't betraying anybody.

They were the ones who'd betrayed *him*. The Old Woman had intended this all along. She'd never meant to give him back his Skin, in spite of all her talk of earning it. Proving it was his. Had Cait known too? Had everybody

163

known, except him, that this was the way it was going to end?

They'd been lying to him from the first.

'I'm not a thief,' he said, thinking, *Not my rules. I didn't make them, so I don't have to play by them. I refuse to be judged by them.*

And all the while he was stumbling forward through frost-rimed heather that wrapped itself around his ankles, trying to trip him up and drag him down. The processional path had been cleared turf, easy walking, welcoming worshippers into the heart of the Ring.

He wasn't walking on it now, and there was no welcome.

It's like those dreams where you try to move and the thing you're trying to get to just keeps on being out of reach and you go on struggling and –

The centre of the Ring, that had seemed so far away, was now, abruptly, right in front of him. The great square hearth, like the hearth he'd sat by with Cait and in every other house in the village, only writ large. He circled the hearth clockwise. He could smell the dung fuel, waiting for the morning. Waiting to be turned into fire.

And when it's blazing, she's going to throw my Silver Skin into it and let it burn.

Well, he wasn't going to just stand by and let that happen – he was going to take back what was his – there – he had it in his hands at last – he was going home – it was going to be all right – it was –

Cait: The Encampment by the Loch of Harray

Cait stirred. Something had woken her. She half-opened her eyes.

What . . .?

Then the scream, furious and full-throated, came again and she was thrashing her way out of the tangle of furs.

'Rab – wake up! Something's happened! Rab! Rab?'

But when she tried to shake his shoulder, the pile of sleeping furs fell in on itself. They had been heaped up to look as if there were someone in amongst them, but it was a lie.

He wasn't there.

And then she was running for the causeway, her heart in her mouth.

Rab: The Ring of Stones

The scream echoed round the Ring, blurred and confusing. Rab clutched the Silver Skin to his chest and spun wildly, trying to pinpoint the source of the sound. For a split second he thought it must the standing stones themselves, crying their outrage.

'Stop – *stop* – sacri – *sacril* – sacrilege—'

The words jumbled and overlapped but he could see figures now, streaming over the causeway, in their hands hastily caught up torches, shockingly yellow in the black-and-white night. A strangled laugh forced its way up his throat as he suddenly thought of pitch-fork-bearing peasants coming for Frankenstein's monster in the old vids.

You're the monster, Rab – you're the monster!

It didn't seem real. He wasted precious seconds thinking, *This doesn't seem real*, before the smell of the torches hit his nostrils – he tasted tin in his mouth – he turned and started to run.

Cait: The Ring of Stones

The causeway was blocked with milling, frightened people, rumpled and only half awake. But Cait could see light and movement from beyond the Stones – Voy and the other Old Women, the Cherts, the Hunters like Tron. Her night vision was spoiled by the torchlight, but she didn't need her eyes to know that there would be someone else, inside the sacred space. Someone who had no right to be there.

You fool – Rab – you fool –

'Let me through! Let me pass!' she yelled.

Bewildered, stupid faces turned and stared and didn't get out of the way until she pushed and shoved.

'What's happened? What's happened?' they bleated. 'What is it? What should we do?'

'Get out of my way,' she snarled. She gritted her teeth and pushed harder – and suddenly she broke through the edge of the crowd and fell sideways against a Stone.

Its rough edge slashed at her, cutting her shoulder and cheek. Moaning softly, she clutched her face and struggled upright, peering into the great circle. Her eyes were drawn to the torch-bearers. The hunters.

And then she saw the prey.

Rab was running. The pursuers had cleared sward under their feet, but he was struggling through uncut heather which clutched at his leggings, the tangled roots trapping his feet. She saw him stagger and lurch.

There was a shout – it was Tron – his anger echoed

strangely off the Stones – Rab hesitated at the sound –
half-turned – and lost his balance.

She watched as he twisted in the air, one arm flung up
– the other clutching something to his chest – she could
see the black circle of his mouth – and then he was gone.
Swallowed up.

Tron's strong legs carried him past the centre of the
Ring and into the heather with relentless speed. When
he reached the place where Rab had fallen he shoved his
hands down like a heron stabbing its beak into the water,
and dragged Rab up. He began to haul him back towards
the centre. Rab had gone limp. She wondered if he was
even conscious.

She wiped the blood from her cheek and walked
towards the centre. There was no reason to hurry now.
What was going to happen next was already decided.
Rab had decided it for himself.

He was going to die.

Voy: The Old Women's Encampment

But Cait was wrong about one thing at least. Voy was not with the pursuers.

She was still at the Old Women's encampment, deep asleep, so deep that Mot gave up calling her and actually started to shake her shoulder. She came awake to discover his tear-stained face inches from her own.

'What a strange dream I was having,' she told him. 'I was flying. What's wrong?'

'I thought you must be dead, when you didn't wake up, and then there would be no one to properly open the Road to the Sun because my mother says you're the only one who's any good at it the rest are just girls compared to you and it's their fault the Sun's so sick and then it'll be dead too and my mother says Tron's going to kill our selkie if you don't come . . .' He ran out of breath at this point, wiped his wet face on his sleeve and jerked out of the way as the Old Woman rose out of her furs like a startled stag surging up out of a hollow.

The crowd before the causeway parted precipitately. For a moment, Voy stood at the entrance to the Ring, watching what was going on inside.

Then she smiled.

It was a sight that made the villagers who saw step back. But then she said, 'All of you. Follow me . . .' and there wasn't a soul who disobeyed.

Rab: The Ring of Stones

'Don't kill him.'

Tron's grip on Rab's tunic had twisted it tight at the neck so he was nearly throttled. The hunter held the Silver Skin in his other hand, two-fingered and at arm's length, so that it hung, limp and bedraggled in the torch light.

'What?' Tron was peering about, trying to locate who had spoken. Rab could smell the rankness of the man's sweat even in the freezing air. He was almost crazy with the desire to kill. Rab was suddenly overwhelmed with the memory of the boar, just a tiny trigger away from a luscious spilling of blood. His blood.

Voy stepped clear of the crowd.

'I said, don't kill him.'

'Why shouldn't I, Old Woman?' Rab felt Tron's grip tighten even further as his hatred found its focus. Each snatched breath was an agony and he scrabbled uselessly at Tron's hand with his nails. The man gave him an impatient shake, like a dog with a rat, and repeated, 'Why shouldn't I kill him?'

'Because you need him.' She sounded patronising, as if Tron were just a little stupid.

'Need *this*?' Tron let go of Rab so suddenly he fell to his knees, crowing for breath. '*We* don't need your fake Fey magic, Old Woman. *We* have something better. We have the Tears of the Sun.'

'Tears of the Sun!' Voy snorted. 'It's called bronze,

Tron. You've got a bit of the new melted rock and, as far as my young Chert tells me, not a particularly good bit at that. Apparently it's got more impurities than you've got nits in that hair of yours. Get your Old Woman to have a word with me, and I can put her in the way of a cure for that. Might even lend her a comb . . .'

The crowd gasped and there was a nervous titter at the back.

Tron flicked a contemptuous finger at Rab, bent double and wheezing. 'And you think *this* – your make-believe selkie boy – can do better?'

'Him?' Voy barely looked at Rab. Her attention was entirely on the hunter. 'No. Not him. It's the skin that's important. Though of course if you kill the human form of a selkie then the skin dies too. I'd have thought everybody knew that.'

Rab staggered to his feet, still struggling to catch his breath. He looked out over the crowd, torch-lit faces open-mouthed, eyes wide, over-excited by the drama being played out in this bizarre theatre.

'A selkie.' Tron snorted. 'How do we know he's not just some back-birth – some freak you've been hiding – Skara Brae runs to freaks – everybody knows *that*.'

'Look at the mark on his arm.' Voy's voice dropped, so that it was deep and mysterious. Everyone edged closer to hear. To see. 'And look at the mark on the skin . . .'

Tron chucked the Silver Skin to one of his men who caught it with evident reluctance.

'Lay it out,' said Voy.

The man did as she told him. He spread the skin on the hearth stone and backed quickly away. *It looks so small,* thought Rab. *Such a little thing.* The damaged sleeve

171

was uppermost. Tron grabbed Rab's arm and dragged it down beside the skin, twisting it so roughly Rab couldn't help crying out. He looked from one to the other for a moment and then he shoved Rab away so that he stumbled and fell again.

'That?' Tron sneered. 'That's nothing. A steady hand and a sharp stick from the fire could have burned that onto the boy. That's no proof he's a selkie.' He raised his voice to reach all of the crowd and said again, 'There's no proof here.'

Rab was aware of bodies shifting and a rustling of disappointment. They wanted more than this. They didn't want the drama to end so soon.

I have to do something . . .

'I can prove it's my Skin,' Rab croaked. *Not loud enough. Everyone has to hear.* He rasped as loudly as he could. 'I can prove the Skin is mine!' He didn't dare look at Voy. *Please, please, let this work . . . please!*

'Well, freak?' Tron's eyes glittered in the torch light. 'How do you think you can do that?'

'Let me hold it.'

Tron grunted suspiciously. 'Why?'

'Because . . . because it will speak to me.' *Please make it so. Please make it so.* 'It will speak to me and to no other person here present.' He realised he was starting to talk like a character in an old vid, but no one else seemed to notice. 'I, er, I challenge you to do as much. Go on, draw the skin over your hand and see if *you* can make it speak.'

He saw the expression on the man's face shift. *You're scared! You bloody bully – you're SCARED!*

'Here, I'll show you—' and Rab reached out for the

172

Silver Skin, but before he could take it, Tron knocked his hand away.

'This is another trick, isn't it, boy?' he snarled. 'You pick up the skin and then *you* speak, but you pretend it's not your voice at all. I've heard of tricksters who can throw their words, so that they seem to come from another place. But let's see how well you do with a gag, eh?' He whipped the greasy strip of leather out of his hair and before anyone could protest, had muzzled Rab tightly.

Rab was terrified he was going to throw up and suffocate in his own sick. He could feel his stomach clenching. *Breathe! Slow breathing, one, two, slower, one . . . two . . . one . . . two . . .*

He managed to calm the gag reflex, until he could look Tron in the eyes again. He could feel how the leather strap had pulled his face into a wide artificial grin. He could see how horrible he looked by the flicker in the man's eyes. It was a tiny satisfaction in amongst all the fear.

No one tried to stop him this time as he stepped forward and picked the Silver Skin up. *Take it carefully, Rab. Slowly.* He slid his bare arm into the undamaged sleeve of the suit. *Please. Com. Please. Talk to me.*

Nothing.

He'd stopped breathing. He felt how every face was turned towards him, with only the deceptive flicker of the torches to show the tremor in their hands.

Please . . .

And then – was that something? Was something happening? And then he was sure – that was it – the cool tingling sensation of the Silver Skin struggling to draw power from his skin. Ever so slightly, the suit began to blur and his dear Com was speaking . . .

'—day, Mayday, can you hear me? C-can you hear me? There's been an accident – seal br-broken – repeat, seal broken – can you hear me?'

And suddenly Cait was standing beside him, crying out loudly, 'Listen, all of you! That's it – that's the language the selkie used when it first came ashore to us. It sounds like gibberish, except for a word here and there – *there!* Did you hear it? It said "seal". And there – again! "Seal" . . .'

'Rab? Rab?'

Everyone heard that.

'It calls him by name!'

'It must be his skin – a real selkie skin!'

'A real selkie!'

Voy stepped forward and dug her claw-like hand into Rab's shoulder.

'That's right, a real selkie,' she said. 'And he's mine.'

Cait: The Ring of Stones

What now? What would they do to him now? She hadn't thought beyond keeping him from being killed. It was like the first day in the fog, on the shore, all over again.

'Take that gag off him,' Voy ordered, pivoting Rab round and propelling him towards Cait. She did as she was told. No one tried to stop her.

How does Voy do that? The thought came into Cait's mind unexpectedly and the envy that came with it was just as unbidden. *Where does she get the power?* Tron felt it – they all felt it – she could see it in the way they stood back, the way the focus of them all was on Voy. All the things Tron had been doing to Rab were things she was *letting* him do. She was in control.

And then Voy began to smile. She took the silver skin from Rab's reluctant fingers. She turned and began to walk towards the standing stones.

'What are you doing?' Cait left Rab and scuttled after her, even took hold of her sleeve. 'Where are you going?' She lowered her voice so no one around them could hear her. 'Look, maybe he's not really a selkie – I didn't tell you – he didn't come from the sea – he fell out of the sky! I didn't tell you because I wasn't sure . . . it didn't make sense . . . I thought I must have got it wrong . . .' *You're lying,* a voice in her head said. *You didn't tell because you wanted her to know less than you did – because what you knew gave you power, over her, over the Old Woman . . .*

But Voy didn't answer. She wasn't listening.

Voy: The Ring of Stones

Voy looked around, suddenly suspicious that these momentous, startling, huge thoughts had taken too much time to form in her mind, and the others would be staring at her, wondering what had frozen her so long. But no. It had happened in a split second. Her mind didn't just feel as if it was racing – it *was* racing.

She detached the girl's hands from her sleeve and pushed her away absently. Everything had been leading to this. This was the moment when she would make everything change. She'd been following the wrong ideas and *in spite of that* they had led her to the perfect place, the only time. Her thoughts were shouting now, so that she could only hear the voices of other people as a buzz in the background, irritating and unimportant as the whirring of insects.

She strode towards the stones.

Rab: The Ring of Stones

There was an appalled gasp from the crowd as Voy reached the ring of stones, turned and began to move around the circle. For a moment Rab couldn't think why they seemed to feel such sudden horror. It wasn't that long ago they'd all been doing the same . . .

Not the same! Not the same!

Voy: The Ring of Stones

She walked the Ring from left to right, widdershins, against the pull of the deosil direction. She spoke words of greeting to each of the great stones – greeting and challenge too, making sure her voice was loud and clear, that however strangely the Ring affected the sound, her words would be heard by the crowd clustered at the centre. She called out to the Sun to listen to her, Voy, to listen and to bring back the Greater Days.

She held the selkie's silver skin in her hands, lifting it high overhead at each stone.

Partway round, she paused and looked back at the people. Their faces were palely visible, there by the great square stone hearth. They seemed far away and insignificant. Voy felt power running through her, making her ruined hands tingle and her old hair stand out from her head. *This is the way it should be. This is the way I am.* She raised the silver skin again and looked up to where the stone met the sky . . .

Rab: The Ring of Stones

Rab ached. It hurt to breathe. He didn't understand what was happening, what Voy was doing, what they were going to do to him, and then, to add to the misery, it started to snow, fat white flakes that landed on him and clung, leeching any tiny remaining warmth from his flesh. He hunched his shoulders, hugging himself. Something in the sky flickered, then rumbled, a low-pitched roar that grew and died away and grew again. He felt it in his bones.

Thunder? In a snowstorm?

It made as much sense as anything. He was too tired now to think. Wearily, he closed his eyes . . .

He might have left them wide open for all the difference it made. When the flash came, the light bored through his eyelids, blinding him. He heard Cait cry out, then the roar came again, pressing down on him, making it hard to think. He couldn't put two and two together – he couldn't draw a conclusion from the evidence and plan ahead, but *Be small! Be unnoticed!* something ancient yammered at him. Rab threw himself to the ground and, with a whimper, covered his head with his arms. For a moment that seemed to last forever, all of his senses fused, overloaded by too much light, too much noise.

The sky has exploded, screamed his mind, and then it shut down.

It wasn't the sky that had exploded – it was the top of the standing stone. The lightning strike split the megalith, so that a slice of rock taller than a man detached and fell, but before it hit the ground the lightning leapt, so quickly it was almost simultaneous, attracted to the next tallest thing. To the Silver Skin, held aloft in the Old Woman's hands.

Voy: The Ring of Stones

Cold. So cold, it burned. She felt her muscles spasm, snapping her spine back in an arc of pain and gripping her chest so she couldn't draw breath. Some force lifted her up into the air, flinging her backwards, awkward and ugly.

No! This wasn't what flying was supposed to be. Hesta had said . . . *No* . . .

She hit the ground so hard she felt her teeth break. There was a roaring inside her head and it was growing louder. As the noise swelled and beat, she looked up into the night sky and saw, suddenly, to her amazement, that it was snowing. Out of the black, drifting down. *No wind,* she thought. *No wind inside the Ring.* She found herself focusing on one snowflake, just one out of the growing crowd. She marvelled at the alien beauty of its construction, tiny and perfect and cold, and at the same time the thought came to her – beyond a shadow of a doubt – that what she was seeing, was death.

If it touches me, I will die.

And then . . . I'll know . . .

And then her peace exploded.

Not yet – not yet – it's not time yet –

Something below her control was having none of it – it was screaming against her life ending – it fought for command over her body, tried to roll it out of the path

181

of the tiny white instrument of death. But as she cried silently to her muscles, there was no answer.

She couldn't move.

Delicately the snowflake drifted down, closer, closer, till with a sigh it settled on her cheek.

Cait: The Ring of Stones

The lightning had split like fingers, one hitting the stone, one striking the hearth at the centre of the Ring. The heat was so great it ignited the huge pile of fuel and offerings, the fire blazing up with a roar, vaporizing the falling snow above with a hiss of steam and lighting the inner faces of the standing stones with a hard white glare. Cait's nostrils were bombarded with the hot reek of seared meat and hide and clay as the offerings were incinerated. But she barely registered any of this. All she saw was the body of the Old Woman, crumpled on the ground.

Rab: The Ring of Stones

'What are you doing?! Stop! You can't just leave!'

It was as if no one could hear him.

Rab had dragged himself to his knees, waiting for someone to rush forward, take command, start resuscitation, bring Voy back ... But no one moved. Seconds passed. Then, as one, they all turned their backs and started to walk away, away from the body on the cold ground, back to the causeway out of the Ring.

They weren't going to do anything to save her. They'd given her up for dead, without even going near her. Even Cait wasn't doing anything more than standing there, holding her snatched-up torch in the hissing snow, her eyes and mouth three black helpless Os in her face.

He didn't know what to do ... It couldn't be up to *him* ...

Come on, Rab, remember what you studied – what do you do first?

His heart clenched in his chest – *Com? Is that you?* – but it was just a memory. The suit was silent and dead, there in the frosted heather where the lightning strike had flung it, glittering like fish scales in the torch-light. But now he remembered – all those First Aid classes – *What Would You Do If No Com Were Nearby*. Everybody'd thought they were just a waste of time, just a joke – in what possible situation would there not be a Com nearby? They'd called it *Anachronism 101*, but it was still compulsory ...

Not me – it can't be up to me!

They were going to let her die.

'NO!'

Rab scrambled through the heather and dropped awkwardly to his knees by Voy's twisted body. Her eyes were wide open but there was no recognition in them. A single snowflake lay on her cheek and it wasn't melting.

'Voy? VOY!' She wasn't breathing . . .

He started pulling at her body, trying to straighten her out. She was limp and unresisting, and he was horrified at the thought that he was manhandling a corpse.

No, I'm not! he told himself fiercely and he tilted her head back and began.

Her mouth was clammy and cold. In the training they'd used porous membranes – there had been no actual mouth-to-mouth contact – it had all been a laugh – he stopped blowing into the Old Woman and pushed on her chest – again – again – again – back to blowing – compressions – blowing – the whole world had shrunk to each action – all time had dwindled into pressures and exhalations and the ragged drawing of the air into his lungs and the pushing of it into hers –

She groaned, rolled over onto her side and vomited.

He heard Cait make a strangled noise and suddenly she was there beside him. She thrust the torch into Rab's hands. She began to feel Voy's arms and legs, wipe her face. It was only then that Rab realised the snow had stopped. He looked up at the sky. The wind was blowing the storm clouds away and there, on the edge of the Ring of Hills, was the setting moon.

It looked so far away, all white and empty and untouched. Unpopulated. Clean.

'What have you done?' murmured Cait.

It was no more than a whisper, but it seemed to Rab to fill the great circle and echo from the stones. *What have you done?*

What have you done?

Cait: The Ring of Stones

The storm passed as quickly as it had come. To the great joy, confusion and, in some cases, fury of the Living, the Road to the Sun opened exactly with the dawn. The spirit stones were emptied, the Dead – the Old Chert of Skara Brae among them – passed on, giving back what they had received.

But who were they to thank?

Tron's Tears? Or the silver skin? Neither of them had been in the inferno of the offering fire. Voy's selkie boy, then? The one who brought her back from death – a road no one had ever walked before? Or had she only slept? Was his Fey skin the thing that had called down fire from the sky? Had they really seen that happen? Already the memories were getting jumbled. The fire from the sky had struck her down, but hadn't killed her. The Stone was split too – there was no doubt about it – but what did that *mean*?

So many questions. The other Old Women pursed their lips, looked solemn and said nothing. They didn't know any more than anyone else, of course. They just weren't letting on.

But Cait had no time for any of that. All her attention was concentrated on dealing with Voy's injuries. Her twisted hands were scorched and blistered. The soles of her feet were burned where the lightning had passed through them as it entered the ground, making small, deep pits in her flesh. And Cait had no way of knowing how much damage it had done inside the Old Woman's body.

At first Voy kept up a low moaning, muttering incomprehensible, frantic sounds, staring wildly about with her bird of prey eyes. The other Old Women shook their heads and didn't understand, but Cait guessed what she wanted. The silver skin lay on the cold ground where it had been flung free. No one wanted to go near it but Cait went and gathered it up. She looked to Rab for permission. He shrugged. He seemed too battered to care.

When she put the skin into Voy's searching hand, the horrible moaning stopped. She clutched it tight to her chest with one arm and was still.

'What was she trying to do out there?' Rab asked Cait, his voice hoarse and weary, but she didn't answer.

Rab: The Ring of Stones

'What was she trying to do?' he'd asked Cait, but the question closest to his heart was, *What has she done?* That was the thing that hammered at his mind and would not give him peace, clawing over and over like a nail in a wound. *What has she done to my Skin?*

He couldn't begin to guess how much damage the suit might have sustained this time. The lightning had passed through Voy's body as well as the Skin – would that mean anything? Would it have provided any kind of buffer or protection? Was his Com online when it happened? If not, where would it have been? How many volts did lightning have? Had the suit and his Com and his only chance of getting a message home been fried, in a second, all of them together, or was there still any hint of hope remaining?

Was this going to be it for him now? Was this, inescapably now, where his life was going to unfold?

He didn't know. He didn't know anything.

Except for one thing. If his chance of getting home had been small before, now it had become microscopic.

PART FOUR

Cait: Return to Skara Brae

The journey back to Skara Brae was silent and slow, beset by sleety winter rain and cruel winds. As Cait watched the villagers through dripping hair, she saw closed faces and bent shoulders.

The men took turns to carry Voy on their backs. She weighed almost nothing, Cait knew – just skin and bones – but each man seemed more than willing to pass the burden on to the next. She saw them wiping their hands surreptitiously on the wet grass afterwards. Some made the sign against evil with their fingers behind their backs.

They'd always feared Voy – of course they had – but this was different.

Rab ventured up to her as they trudged along. 'Has she said anything yet?' he asked.

Cait shook her head fiercely, and he backed away at once.

She was too unsettled to talk.

She'd never seen anyone ill in this way before, which wasn't surprising, since she'd never seen anyone come back from the dead before either. It was as if Voy had become split down the middle into two people, one of which was still dead, while the other was alive. One side of her face was waxy and grey, all the wrinkles strangely flattened away, and yet the other side scowled and glared, with all the malevolent glitter in the depth of the eye that there had ever been. One arm flopped, limp and uncontrolled – one foot would not bear her weight when they tried to stand her on the ground – and yet the other hand and foot were as they'd been before.

What does it mean? What should I do?

There was nothing *to* do, except keep walking through the rain. Get her back to Skara Brae. Get her warm, and dry, and then . . .

Wait and see.

But the other thing that made her mind feel like a cornered rabbit, twitchy and unsure, leaping first in one direction and then just as wildly in another, was what had happened at the Ring.

She didn't understand it. None of it.

Voy will have to explain it, she thought. *Voy's the one who'll know.*

But Voy was saying nothing.

At no point on the journey had Voy let the silver skin go. Back in her own house, it was the same. When Cait laid the Old Woman's flaccid body down onto the heather and hide of her bed and covered her with fleeces, the suit lay with her like a desiccated twin.

Even in the few days they'd been away, the house had grown cold and damp. Cait lit the fire, building it up with dung and dried seaweed until it was strong enough to heat water. She put herbs on to brew – fennel for strengthening, garlic for internal healing, bog myrtle to call back Voy's mind, crowberry to cast out the chill . . . She was just guessing, but there was no one to ask. She raised Voy and held the cup for her to drink, though even then, half the liquid dribbled out of the dead side of her mouth. She heated stones in the fire and wrapped them carefully in soft hide and put them at the Old Woman's

194

feet. She chafed her hands with her own warm ones, trying to bring the life back into them.

It was like chafing the hands of a corpse.

A night and a day passed, and still Voy did not speak.

Rab had been staying out of the way, sleeping she didn't know where, but now he ducked into the house. He hunkered down on the other side of the hearth and looked at her, his brown eyes wide and enquiring.

'Is she . . .?' he asked.

Cait snapped, 'Is she better? Is she worse? Is she the same? *I* can't tell. I've done everything I can think of, but this isn't a sickness I know.' She closed her eyes. 'Sorry.' He was just asking, but it felt like one burden more than she could bear.

'I think it's a stroke,' said Rab.

But what help was a name? He admitted he didn't know what you were supposed to *do* when somebody had this thing, this stroke, any more than she did.

'I think you need special neural stimulators and brain pathway re-routers to heal it,' he said, 'so even if we knew that was what it was, we couldn't . . .' His words trailed away, and he stared into the fire.

Cait looked at him sidelong. He hadn't talked strange like that for such a long time. The events of the Ring of Stones had changed him as well as the Old Woman. Everyone was changed except her. She was just the same. Angry and betrayed and twitchy.

Her skin itched.

Her skin itched. Then why was *he* scratching?

'They say there's bad weather coming,' he said, ratching his nails across the scar on his arm in a way that made her

195

want to hit him. 'The sky's gone all weird. Sketh's been yelling at Mewie ever since we got back – you can hear it all over the village.'

Cait shrugged. 'He's scared we've all forgotten how important he is. If he could get about, he'd be kicking and cuffing everyone, just to remind them. At the moment, Mewie's the only one he can reach.'

Rab pulled a face. 'It's not fair.'

'What's the point of saying things like that? Things aren't fair. Things just are.' Cait shifted. That didn't sound like her. That sounded like everybody else, but not her.

Rab was rubbing hard between his eyes. 'My head feels like it's a size too small. And my skin – it feels all crawly. Why is that?'

Cait didn't answer. It was true, she too felt a pressure in her skull and that sense of invisible bugs creeping over her . . . She stood up abruptly. 'Stay with Voy,' she snapped and headed for the door.

'No – but – wait—' began Rab, looking appalled, but it was too late.

She'd gone.

Rab: Skara Brae

'You. Come here.'

It was her. The Old Woman.

Rab gulped. 'You're . . . but . . . Cait just left . . . I'll go and get her—'

'No. You.' Her voice sounded gravelly. Different. The words were a little slurred. But there was no mistaking the old authority. Rab sidled over to the bed box. He had to force himself to look inside.

The Old Woman was lying there with her ghastly twisted face, staring at him.

'Sit me up.'

He desperately did not want to touch her. He did it anyway. She seemed to weigh nothing at all, as if her bones were hollow, like a bird's. When he had settled her against the end of the bed she spoke again. 'Now,' she said. 'You're going to tell me.'

'Tell you . . .?'

'Who you are.'

Rab drew in a breath sharply, but before he could start to protest, the Old Woman made an abrupt chopping action with her hand.

'Don't . . . lie to me. I don't have . . . time.'

He looked into her mismatched eyes and knew it was a fact. She was dying. What he'd done at the Ring, bringing breath back into her body and re-starting her heart, had only put death off a matter of days. She had very little time left, and in the time she had, she was suffering.

Maybe it was no kindness, bringing you back. Maybe I shouldn't have interfered . . .

'You're not a selkie.' It wasn't a question. 'You're . . . like the piper.'

'Er . . .' He knew he was looking stupid and shifty. He could see it made her angry. And with her anger came new strength.

'You heard the story. Of the piper. Who went into the trows' hill. *You* went into a hill and time folded. You came out with trow treasure. That's what the skin is. That's what you are. The piper.'

The story. Rab remembered old Benth telling the story in the paved place one warm afternoon – about the piper who was lured into a hill and in the morning hundreds of years had passed and everyone he knew was long dead.

'You're from the past,' said Voy.

Rab's hands were sweating. 'Why do you think that?'

'Don't play with me, boy. I think it because there's nothing left *to* think.' She closed her eyes and her face looked like a skull in the dim light. Her voice rasped on. 'You're going to tell me how things used to be. In the Greater Days. You're going to tell me where we went wrong.'

'I'm not from the past . . .' He tried to hedge, slide past the truth, but she made another angry, impatient gesture and suddenly he found himself saying, 'I'm from the future.'

The space under the turf roof filled with sudden, appalled silence. Rab couldn't think, couldn't breathe. Couldn't believe he'd just said what he'd just said. How had it happened – how had she made him say those words?

198

There was a look of triumph on her twisted face. 'There is a future . . . there is a future . . . tell me!'

And so Rab found himself having with Voy the conversation he had denied himself again and again, the conversation he'd longed to have with Cait. He was telling her the truth – about everything – about who he was and where he'd come from – when he'd come from – the Silver Skin, his Com, the accident . . . He filled the little time she had left with talk of time, great swathes of time, stretching out into the far, distant future. It was the one thing he had sworn not to do and he was doing it anyway.

He couldn't tell how much of it she was understanding – and his explanations weren't always all that clear – but she asked no questions. She just let him talk.

And even as he spoke, he feared he'd been right to keep silent before. He'd thought it would be such a relief but instead it felt somehow bitter . . . dangerous. As if by telling the future he was killing it, or making it something else, something strange. Something wrong. Every mistake he made, through ignorance or poor memory, would be made real, just by the action of his voice in this hut on this island in the cold northern sea.

You're so stupid, he told himself scornfully. *You think you just open your yap and the rest of history's going to roll over and play dead? When did somebody die and make YOU God?!*

It didn't help.

It didn't help that there was so much he didn't know. All those years of study and he'd barely begun to learn. It didn't help that of the things he *did* know there was so much he just couldn't explain properly. He had an

199

Alexander Decision Age mouth, and the Old Woman had Stone Age ears.

He muddled on, trying not to backtrack too much, trying to make things that were intensely complex sound simple and straightforward until he became so tangled his words just died away . . .

'How do you know all this?' she said into the silence. 'We can barely remember from one cycle to the next.'

So he explained written language. Badly. Until he suddenly remembered the cryptic scratchings in the passageway and along the stone edge of her bed box. He pointed to them. She listened with such hunger.

'You know everything, from all the world's time. Nothing is ever lost . . .'

Rab stared at her. What in all the garbled muddle of his words had given her that idea? 'No – no – so *much* is lost! But there are people who want to know and they ask questions. Even when they might never know the answers, they keep on asking questions. That's why I came here. Except . . . it went wrong.'

'Except you're stuck here now and can't tell anybody the answers.'

'No. NO! I'm going to get back. I'm going to get home.' But his voice cracked as he said it.

'And then you'll tell them all about us.'

Rab hung his head. 'I don't know all about you.'

'That's right. You don't,' the Old Woman murmured.

But Rab didn't hear her. He was overwhelmed by a picture in his mind of him trying to describe and explain and make real Skara Brae and Voy and Sketh and Mewie and the Ring – and Cait – to the people of his own time, and the harder he tried to imagine it the less possible it became. Out of his words they would only see primitive housing and pagan rituals and people who smelled and bashed stones together and believed in fairy stories. They would say, 'That's interesting. Fascinating to know. Great to have the questions answered. You must be desperate to get sanitized, right?'

No matter how hard he tried to explain, he would fail. And in spite of all he *had* learned, he still wouldn't know the most important answer of all. He still wouldn't know *what had happened at Skara Brae*. Sometime, some thousands of years in its future, some thousands of years in his past, Skara Brae had been found. Uncovered by a ferocious storm. But when had it disappeared under the sand? Were there people trapped in their houses when the time came? Did they all die, suffocating on grit – or were they long gone, the village already deserted like the others Mot had told him about, when the dunes came and buried the houses? Why didn't he know *that*? Everything he'd been telling Voy seemed pointless. It meant less than the salt smell of the seaweed burning in the hearth. Less than the sound of the wind in the sky or the ache in his legs.

He buried his head in his hands.

'So,' she said in a harsh whisper. 'So. There are children of time after all – and grand-children too.'

'What?'

'Never mind.' She waved his puzzlement aside. She leaned back, propped against the hard stone, never blinking. Her lop-sided smile was terrible to look at. He had to remind himself that she couldn't help the way only half of her face moved, but it was as if two separate personalities were peering out at him, one that stared with such icy, blank evil, the other grinning with some kind of manic delight. Both of them making his skin crawl . . .

He couldn't look at her any more. He let his head drop into his hands again.

'Are you going to tell Cait?' he said, his voice muffled and weary.

Voy didn't answer. Her breathing sounded troubled again, as if she were struggling with something, but he didn't look up. And then . . .

'Well?' she said. 'Don't you want it?'

'Want what?' What could he possibly want, except maybe to sleep for a year?

It wasn't sleep she was offering him.

It was his Silver Skin.

Cait: Skara Brae

She straightened just outside the entranceway to the paved place and paused. Sketh's muffled voice came along the passageway behind her, berating his patient wife, reasserting his authority like a midden cock pecking at the hens. Mostly everyone was staying in their own houses, quietly doing the chores that a few days' absence had built up. Keeping out of sight. Keeping their heads down. The strangeness of the times wasn't their problem. It was for people like the Old Woman to sort through, not them.

Only Ailth had come, like her, to look at the sky.

'No birds,' he grunted. 'No wind and no birds.' His breath puffed white from his mouth.

He was right. The sky hung low over the village, muddy with clouds. There was no wind stirring the grass and no bird crying from the shore. The cold bit at the skin of her face, making her flinch.

Cait had never known weather like this. She was about to ask Ailth what could it mean, when she stopped. She saw the way he was watching her. It was a strange look, a waiting look.

He's expecting something – from me. Answers. What does he think I know?

'Ailth. Help.'

He lifted one shoulder. 'I can't.'

'You can.'

And then he opened his arms.

*

When she left him, Ailth lay still in the darkness of the Stone Maker's house. He'd never known her like that before. It was as if her body had been trying to speak directly to his, no, more than speaking – shouting. He'd have bruises to show for it, he knew that for certain.

Maybe it was the coming storm?

Cait crept up the long passageway and turned towards home. She felt light, as if she had bird bones. *As if I could fly. Fly away.* She came through the doorway and straightened – and there was Rab with the silver skin dangling woefully in his hands.

'Look – she . . . she gave it to me! And then she just fell asleep. And her breathing sounds awful—'

Rab: Skara Brae

For so long, all his thoughts had been bent towards the moment he got the Silver Skin back. And now he had it, or what was left of it, and all he felt was confusion and doubt. He ran his fingers over the damaged material and the ripped helmet. There was no knowledge in this time that could repair them, and even if there were, the necessary materials didn't exist. He had a sudden mental picture of Cait sewing up the tatters of the silver skin with gut thread and patches of hide and decorating the jagged neckline with pierced shells and red-ochre clay beads.

He was aware of her watching him from behind her veil of hair. He was aware of Voy, suddenly awake again, watching from the bed box, each breath painful to listen to. One of these women knew so much about him and, in spite of all he'd just told her, it wasn't the old one.

'Cait . . . I . . .'

'There's a storm coming,' said Cait in a flat voice. 'It will be bad.'

'I'll just . . . I'm just going to . . .'

She turned away. He loved the way her neck showed where her pale hair had fallen forward. It was grubby and so familiar it made his heart clench.

Voy was still watching. He bent down and crawled out along the passageway. In the low cramped space he stopped and took a deep breath. In spite of the cold, he found his hands were sweating as he pulled the undamaged sleeve of the Silver Skin onto his arm. The singed remains of the suit dangled awkwardly. Was his Com still in there? Could it have survived? He felt again the tingling feeling on his skin as the suit struggled for some power, but was it fainter this time?

He realised he was, pointlessly, holding his breath, and let it out in a whoosh that was close to a sob.

Come on, come on, come ON . . . Are you there?

And then he got an answer.

'—ab? Rab? Oh, I feel *t-terrible*—'

'Com? Com!'

'Rab, is that you?'

'Com.' The tears rolled down Rab's face, sudden and hot and surprising.

'It – it's you! You're alive! Oh, R-Rab, something awful has happened. I think we c-crashed, and then I think I was activated and then the power was gone again and could we POSSIBLY have been hit by LIGHTNING? and it's not 1850, and, and . . .'

'It's all right,' said Rab, grinning and wiping the tears from his face. 'I know.'

Speaking Standard again after so long felt strange. Rab did his best to tell his Com the basic facts of what had happened, but it was clear that it was only able to take in a little of what he was saying. The amount of power it could draw from the sleeve of the suit was only enough for some of its most basic functions.

'You have to understand – these people – they're . . . I mean to me they're . . .'

'Understand . . .' said his Com. 'Understand?' It really didn't know what he was talking about – how could it?

You weren't here, he thought desperately. *You don't understand – you don't know –*

He felt sick.

No one would understand.

He pushed the thought away.

'Should I put the suit on properly now? See how much power I can give you?'

His Com squawked in alarm. 'No-no-no-no, not here! We have to wait . . . wait for the l-last minute, Rab. I can't guarantee there'll be no more . . . fire.' It whispered the last word as if it were afraid, and Rab shuddered. 'Get d-down to the shore, Rab – you need to, to, be as close to your original entry point . . . as posssssssible.'

'Leave?' Rab stared stupidly down at his arm. 'You want me to leave?'

'What is it saying, your skin?'

Cait had come along the passageway to him. She put a lit clay lamp on the ground between them. The bones of her face, lit from below, were strangely sharp and angular. Rab was ashamed of himself for having jumped at the sound of her voice.

I feel so guilty! Why do I feel so guilty?

'It's not the skin talking – it's the . . . No, never mind, my, er, skin – it's saying I have to leave. Now. Right away.' It was impossible to read her face in the eerie light. *Help! I don't know what to do!* he thought at her. *What do you want me to do?*

Nothing. She was giving him nothing.

'Are you sure about this – leaving right away, I mean?' he havered to his Com. 'There's a storm coming – nobody's going to be able to find us in bad weather – it's going to be a bad one.' He lowered his voice. 'Don't you

207

remember – it was a storm that got us into this mess in the first place!' Unconsciously, he rubbed the puckered scar, his dread growing with the touch. Red pain, heat, his body pulsing . . . 'I don't think this is a good time to leave.'

'Need, need, the storm,' his Com insisted. 'Need an anchor point – something big . . . noticeable . . . too much of time is too hom-hom-ogenous. Too much all the same. They could miss you by weeks – years – need something significant . . .'

Rab thought of all the time here, all the upheaval, all the emotion. *Not significant*. He gave a small grimace.

'You're happy because you're leaving, aren't you.' Cait's voice was dangerously calm.

'I wasn't *smiling*. I mean I was, but not like that. I'm not leaving. Not yet, I mean. The suit, I mean my skin, is too damaged. But if I can use it to send a message to my people, then . . .'

Guilt came crawling up his throat again.

'I'm just going to send a message and then I'm coming back – I'll be here to help with the storm . . .' He didn't know what else to say and shrugged helplessly.

'I don't need your help. Just leave.' She spat the words so fiercely he shuffled backwards involuntarily. She went on talking, low and harsh and angry. 'You go back to your people, your world, put on your tatty silver skin that's done nothing but cause trouble for us – *nothing!* – just like the stories, and you'll forget any of it ever happened. You'll leave and you'll forget us, and me, and you'll forget . . .'

Rab shook his head. 'Never. I . . . never . . .' He was overwhelmed with a warmth, a tenderness that made tears burn in his eyes. He didn't know where he was going to die, but he knew without a shadow of doubt that when the time came, he would still remember the feel of her skin against his, the sound of waves on sand and the smell of burning seaweed, the tiny specks of gold in the depths of her eyes.

'I won't forget you because that would be like forgetting myself. And if you don't believe me, you're just as stupid as . . . as Sketh! And anyway – I'm coming back and that's a promise.'

He leaned over to kiss her mouth but she turned her head at the last moment and he kissed her hair instead. It tasted of salt. Her smell was rich and complicated and achingly familiar.

I don't want to go! he thought and the thought was so clear and strong he felt as if he'd screamed it out loud.

Rab didn't want to go, but he went anyway. He didn't want her to see the tears on his face.

He didn't see the tears on hers.

Cait: Skara Brae

'He's gone then.' Voy's harsh whisper came out of the shadows as Cait re-entered the house.

Cait hid her face in her hair. 'He said he'd come back,' she muttered.

'He's gone. He won't come back.'

Cait felt her shoulders sag. The Old Woman was right, of course. Selkies never returned.

I'm so tired. Why am I so tired, all of a sudden?

'Move me to the fire,' the Old Woman whispered.

She made a nest of hides by the hearth and settled Voy into it. The Old Woman looked more than ever like a malignant toad.

'Heat . . . heat water. Bring me my bag of herbs.'

It was hard for the Old Woman to handle the little sacks of medicines, but she snarled angrily when Cait tried to help. She bent herself over the herbs and the cup, hiding what she was doing, glaring over at Cait from time to time with her mismatched eyes.

Like a buzzard hunched over a dead rabbit. Keep your secrets, old woman. I don't want them.

'Take my bed out.' Strange sounds crowded closer around Voy's words, but she pushed the sense past them. 'Take it. Out.'

She sounds like the voice in Rab's skin. Perhaps it had a stroke too. But it made her chest ache to think about Rab.

Selkies never come back.

Cait pushed the thoughts away and did what Voy said. She laid aside the fleeces and hides. She lifted out the heather mattress, thinking as she did so that it would need renewing soon. *It's a good thing I brought in the fresh heather before all that rain,* she thought. But most of her mind was numb.

'Lift the slab.'

'What?'

'Do. Do it.'

Cait bent down and felt along the stone floor of the bed. It seemed unbroken, even though she knew Rab had found the way to open it. That seemed so long ago now, but it hadn't been any time at all.

'A notch.'

Cait felt again. Yes, there it was – a gap she could get her fingers into.

'Open it.'

Suddenly, there was nothing but horror in her mind. Whatever was under that slab had been trapped, pinned by the fifth spirit stone, all the years of her life, unable to escape. *It's my mother,* she told herself. *It's my mother.* But she couldn't steady her breathing or stop the sweat from making her hands slick.

'Open it!' There was no denying that harsh whisper. There was no escaping the Old Woman.

Cait forced her fingers into the gap and put her weight behind raising the stone.

At first it resisted, and then, suddenly, something gave way and she was able to tip the slab up and lean it against the wall side of the bed.

It was dark in the space below.

Cait took a branch of the heather and lit it at the hearth.

She paid no attention to the Old Woman now. It was as if she were alone in the house. Her heart beat unsteadily in her chest and her hand shook as she held the spitting heather branch high and looked into the stone cist.

In the flickering light the skeleton lying at the bottom of the cist seemed to move. Shreds of rotted clothing tangled between the white bones, and there, wedged amidst the ribs, was the fifth spirit stone.

And Cait found that all the fear had vanished, and only pity remained.

'Mother.'

Her hand was steady as she reached down, gently freed the spirit stone from the cage of ribs, and lifted it out. She dropped the stone gently onto the floor and let it roll away. She heard the words of release that the Old Woman murmured, but it didn't matter. She didn't need them. She was free. They were both free.

'There,' she said softly. 'There.'

A flare of reddish colour at the body's throat caught the light. Cait leaned closer and then gasped. Her mother was wearing an entire necklace of amber. Cait had never seen so many, so fine pieces of the precious stuff in her whole life, let alone all in the possession of one person.

'She must have been a great lady,' she murmured in awe.

Voy grunted. 'Because of the necklace? Who knows – maybe every child in her land cuts its teeth on amber. Anyway, it's yours now. The cord will have perished long since. Take a new length and thread them, before they get lost.'

Cait nodded. Gently, as if she were afraid of waking

her mother, she lifted out each of the pieces of amber from among the bones and threaded them onto a fresh length of leather. When it was done she tied the cord and lifted the necklace over her head. It clunked against the necklace Mewie had given her. She was surprised at how light it felt, lying on her chest. She cradled the great central piece in her hand and felt it warm to her touch, and looked again into the cist.

Cait didn't know how long she stayed like that, looking quietly down at the bones of her mother. Only gradually did she become aware of the noise in the roof. It was the wind. The uneasy quiet had passed. The storm was rising. Her thoughts automatically reached out to Rab, then pulled back abruptly at the sharp pain.

It was still too new, too raw. He was gone. She wondered when she would get used to it. *They don't tell you in the stories, how long it hurts. How long you go on looking out to sea, and hoping.*

She gave herself a shake. She'd spent her whole life dreaming of this moment. This was when her real life could finally begin. She could walk away from all the old constraints. She could walk away from Skara Brae and go in search of her own people, her own village. She would turn her back and walk away and never, ever come back, because no one could make her do it. No one could make her do anything, ever again. That's what being free was about. Being able to walk away.

As soon as the storm is over . . . as soon as it's over . . .

Meantime, there was work to be done, here and now. She turned to Voy. 'The storm's getting close. Shall I tell them to prepare?'

'Tell them what you like. It's not my problem.' Voy

213

drew a rattling breath and then said something that made Cait's heart jerk into her throat.

'You're the Old Woman now,' Voy said.

For a moment, Cait thought she was going to be sick. As if a hard heavy stone was pressing down on her chest, pinning her there, trapping her. *No. No, please, no.*

'What did you say?' she whispered, swallowing hard to get the words past the bitter taste in her mouth.

Voy didn't bother to repeat her words. She knew she didn't need to.

'No! NO!' Cait's whisper grew to a shriek. 'I don't want – I never wanted—' *You're tying me to them forever! This isn't my release – the Old Woman can't go away, can't find her real village, her real people.* 'You can't make me!'

A horrible wheezing, rasping sound cut through her words.

It was Voy, laughing at her. She held the cup cradled between her live hand and her dead one. Cait wrenched the cup from her, but it was too late. It was already empty.

'*What was in that drink?*'

'Corncockle.'

One word, dropped into the space between them like a stone into a pool of black water. A crackling word, a silly-sounding word.

It made Cait's blood go cold.

Rab: Bay of Skaill

'I hope you've been keeping notes, Rab – you'll be up for a bloody penthouse on the back of all this awfulness! This terrible experience – what you've had to endure – I can't begin to imagine.'

Keeping notes . . . all this awfulness . . . terrible experience . . . endure . . . Rab heard the echo of his own voice saying words just like that, but now they sounded like someone else. They didn't sound like him.

He remembered being so frustrated at not having recording equipment – so fed up that he wasn't going to be able to remember half of the detail . . . He knew now there was nothing he would forget. Ever.

Clutching the Silver Skin in his arms, Rab ran for the shore. Nervous twists of wind threw grit in his eyes and then disappeared into the cold marram grass. There was a metallic taste to the air. Directly overhead, the sky was heavy, like a stone weighing down on the world.

I just . . . I just need to let them know I'm all right. It's the right thing to do – let them know – then explain how I can't go back, not just yet. It's only fair – they'll have been worrying about me all this time . . .

Or would they? Hadn't he already interfered, by being here, by letting Voy get her hands on the Silver Skin, by telling her who he really was? Maybe he'd already changed time. Maybe it was already too late.

So what if I end up being my own great-great-great-grandfather, or whatever's supposed to happen. I don't care. I'm staying, till I know what happens next.

Even if it means you never existed? The question forced its way into his head.

That's not going to happen.

You don't know that.

All right. I DON'T know.

But that didn't change his mind. He wasn't going to run away in the middle of a crisis. But was it a crisis? THE crisis? Maybe at some point in the future, they all just moved away. Found someplace nicer to live. Went off to find Cait's people, maybe – found them, intermarried, all that, lived happily ever after . . .

Maybe the village had been deserted for years when the sand filled it in? A great storm uncovered Skara Brae in 1850. But what storm buried it in the first place? A coast like this, unprotected from thousands of miles of open ocean and its winds – it must change constantly. Slowly and then, sometimes, drastically. A storm could take all the sand between Skara Brae and the sea and dump it on the houses, enough to bury them completely. Bury the houses and everything they contained. Everyone they contained.

But was that what happened? Was that what was *about* to happen? There were storms all the time here. The islands were like a magnet for bad weather. There was no reason to think this was THE storm, the one that buried Skara Brae for thousands of years.

But what if it was?

I'll go to the shore and get a message home and then I'll come back and somehow, somehow, make Cait and the others leave Skara Brae. I'll think of something. I can't just let them die, smothered, suffocated in sand.

216

His Com was not going to be happy, but it wasn't his Com's call.

He didn't care about the thing – the Non-Intervention Contract – he'd signed, promising not to interfere. He'd been another person then.

I'll go home – of course I'll go home – but just not NOW – not if this is THE storm – not knowing what I know . . .

As he panted towards the shore, he said to himself again and again, *But it's not this storm . . . it's not this storm . . .*

At the top of the dunes he stopped and stared. The dark line of seaweed and flung flotsam that marked the furthest reaches of the tide had disappeared. Greasy swells crawled across the bay. Their motion only seemed slow – as he watched he saw how quickly they worked their way up the beach. It was like a tide that had forgotten how to turn. It was like a tide that was determined to eat the world. He looked out to sea. An angry purple bruise was spread across the horizon, bulging up into the sky. Sullen sheets of lightning glared across it.

Any hope that he'd had, died then. The storm that was coming was no ordinary storm. History was about to happen.

Cait: Skara Brae

There was no poison more feared. Corncockle grew among the barley fields, a deadly snare for the unwary. There was no cure.

'Why? Voy, why?'

'Because it's time.' The Old Woman's words cut through the crowding strange sounds that tried to suffocate them. They cut through the rising ruckus of the storm. Sweat stood out on her twisted face with the effort of speech, as she fought doggedly for each syllable. 'Because I choose not to be just another Benth, just another extraneous crone. Because I choose to be remembered for ever.'

And then she laughed, even though that too was a cruel effort.

'Don't you see?' She reached out her working hand and dug her fingers into Cait's arm. They felt like the claws of an eagle. 'I choose to be the question they ask – the children of time – long after the likes of Sketh and Tron – and you – have passed out of mind. They'll ask – about me – and they won't find the answer—'

And then there was only enough energy left for her to laugh with. She let go of Cait's arm and cackled and wheezed.

A sudden gust of wind shook the roof. Dirt trickled down, making the fire stutter. Without thinking, Cait reached over to mend it, but Voy shook her head.

'Leave it. It's time. Make my bed.'

Cait reached for the stone to cover the cist.

'No!'

'What? I don't understand.' But she did.

'There!' Voy pointed, jabbing the air with her finger. 'Make my bed there!'

Cait's heart juddered in her chest. Voy was telling her to make her bed in the cist, beside the empty bones. The two women who had given Cait life, lying side by side, one dying, one dead. *But then,* she thought, *why not?* There was no horror there in the cist. Her mother was at rest. Her bones wouldn't mind the company.

Voy pointed again. 'There.'

Cait began to work, just as she'd done hundreds of times before. She laid fresh heather down, plumping it up to make a fragrant, springy mattress. She smoothed the supple hide over it, carefully tucking it in at the edges. She shook the fleece, hard, to make the wool stand up and dislodge any vermin, and laid it to one side.

The drug in the drink had almost finished its work. The glitter in the Old Woman's eye was dimming at last. *Except she's not the Old Woman – I am. Me.* She almost felt like laughing, it was so ridiculous.

'*Now.*'

Cait lifted her. It was no effort – such a little weight. She carried her from the dying hearth and laid her down in the cist, her last strange resting place.

The Old Woman sighed, as if in contentment. Then she reached over and lightly placed her live hand over the bony hand of the other woman. It was a gentle gesture, almost loving.

And then she was gone.

Cait laid the fleece over them both. As she stepped

219

back, she kicked against something loose on the floor. It was the spirit stone that had been missing from the shelves for so long. She bent, picked it up and put it back in its place beside the others.

There was a scratch at the door. When she opened it, Ailth was there. He didn't speak. He just looked at her and waited.

'Voy is dead,' Cait said. 'Tell the others.'

Ailth nodded and backed away, carefully keeping his gaze away from whatever mysteries the house of the Old Woman might contain.

Cait pulled the door stone across again and waited. It was not long before the scratch came again, and again she pulled the door stone aside.

They were all there, all the villagers, crouched in the passageway. Above the growing whine of the wind, Cait could hear Sketh swearing steadily somewhere at the back of the crowd – *I'll be needing to take the stitches out soon,* she thought in an oddly calm part of her mind – but everyone else was silent. Their eyes glittered in the torch light. They were watching her. No, they were *looking to* her.

The amber of her mother's necklace flickered in the torch light, a deep red circle round her throat. She could feel it warm against her skin. She could see the impact of it registering in the faces of the villagers.

'Voy is dead,' she told them.

They nodded, accepting. Not surprised.

'The storm that is coming is not an ordinary one,' she told them.

They knew that too.

'This is what I have decided we should do . . .' As she

220

gave her instructions, she waited for the outrage, the disdain, the opposition. The cries of *Why should we listen to YOU? What right have YOU to tell us what to do?*

But the cries did not come.

Rab: Bay of Skaill

'Put on the suit, Rab – there's not enough power.'

There was no point in arguing when his Com was still so weak. He began to strip off. He laid aside the wool and hide that had felt so alien at first, placing them carefully in a dip in the sand beside the Silver Skin. For a cold, shuddering instant, he was between worlds, between times – not tied to any. Then he reached for the suit. He dragged it on, ripping it even further in the process. He could see his own brown skin through the tears.

Will it work with the seal broken? Can it generate enough power to send a message all that way? So far into the future?

The sky felt lower every time Rab glanced up, as if a malicious force were pushing down a lid. The boiling of black clouds from the sea drew closer, growing percpetibly. They were hypnotic to watch, so mesmerizing he jumped in surprise when his Com's voice suddenly spoke. It sounded like a shout, but it was only going through a check list of things to do, consider, calculate . . .

Rab felt a sudden wave of affection. *I've missed you!*

'—narrow the band width – no more than 6.e units to the vertical degree – to have any chance – with the storm as an anchor, surely that would . . .'

The stuttering was gone, now that his Com had more energy to draw on, but the damage to the suit was clearly affecting it still. Rab could tell it was having to struggle

222

with all the calculations necessary to send a message through the reluctance of time, measurements and equations which normally would have only given it delight. But he had to talk to it. He had to make it understand the situation.

'Com? As soon as the message is sent, I have to go back to the village. Are you listening? I have to go back to the village and warn them that this is a really serious storm . . .' He found his words trailing off.

His Com wasn't listening.

'A storm – yes – perfect – that's our marker – that's how they'll find us—'

'Com?'

'We need to be higher. There's too much vertical discrepancy.'

'All right – higher – but we'll have to hurry so I can . . . Com? Talk to me!'

'Not – now – Rab—'

Rab took a ragged breath, trapped between doubt and the crushing sky and the swelling sea and that wall of clouds blooming up like a great black rose on the horizon. Then he started to run. He pounded along the curve of the bay, splashing through searching fingers of white foam, towards the north headland where the chambered cairn clung at the edge of the cliff. There wasn't time to go back to where the path started the incline. He'd have to cut up, straight from the beach.

The Silver Skin buzzed in the charged air. His feet thwapping into the wet sand sounded unnaturally loud. It felt wrong to be making so much noise. It felt wrong to be drawing attention . . .

Rab reached the first spray-wet rock. The seaweed

splayed across it glowed, a lurid unnatural green, like something noxious.

Higher – must get higher –

He didn't dare look behind him now. Placing his feet with all the care he could manage, he scrambled from one sharp boulder to the next. If he could just get to the top of the headland . . . He could *feel* the deep roaring of the storm now, vibrating in the rock before it even reached his ears. Wicked little gusts of wind tried to knock him sideways, but he kept low and climbed on.

'It's working . . . is it working? . . . Mayday! Mayday? . . .' his Com whittered.

Rab's breath was coming in sobs – there wasn't enough air – it was wrong – everything was wrong –

There was slick grass under his hands now. He looked up and saw the domed shape of the cairn above him, showing dark against the grey sky. It crouched on the end of the headland like a sullen watchdog.

Higher . . . higher . . .

Each scrambling step was becoming harder to take. The flattened top of the headland came so suddenly he found himself still crawling forward when he could now stand. His Com was urging him on, and all he knew for sure was that he was going away from what he wanted, from what meant the most to him, away from -

And then it happened. Suddenly he knew he was no longer alone.

'NO! – WAIT!—'

Unseen hands grasped his arms.

He struggled wildly. 'I only wanted to send a message – I have to go back – you don't understand – wait! – I can't leave them *now* – I can't leave her now – I have

224

to go back—' For a brief moment he managed to break free from the invisible rescuers from the future and scrabbled sideways, back towards the edge of the headland. He slid on the wetness of the grass, almost fell down the steep drop, down onto the rocks. With a huge effort, he dragged himself upright.

'No more damage!' his Com was wailing. 'No more damage!'

And the storm hit, a wall of black, screaming wind and cloud, slashed through with lightning, battering at the sea, throwing it into the air, devouring the land. Rab struggled to keep his feet as he stared desperately towards the village and Cait.

It was gone. She was gone. The wind had hit the sand of the shore and was peeling it away in swathes – walls of grit, flung inland with terrifying force.

'Cait.' Rab's voice was less than a whisper as the unseen hands caught hold of him again, sealing the rends in the Silver Skin, drawing a helmet over his head, over his face, blinding him. 'Cait . . .'

And then there was no one, and nothing, but the wind.

Mrs Trevelyan: mid Victorian Age, Bay of Skaill, Orkney

'Quite a storm,' said Mr Trevelyan.

Mrs Trevelyan nodded calmly. Her husband disliked fuss. He would be displeased to learn his new young wife had spent so much of the night awake. And he would *certainly* disapprove if she mentioned that she'd heard the shrieking of lost souls in the howls of the wind or that the hiss of blown sand against his house had made her skin crawl.

So she did *not* mention these things, and Mr Trevelyan went on speaking, his voice measured and, as always, slightly too loud.

'The inclement weather was the result of what is referred to as a neap tide, made more extreme by the phase of the moon, which is at the full, combined with a particularly strong westerly wind off the Atlantic. There is, as I may have mentioned to you before, no land mass between our beach and the Americas that might alleviate the force of storm fronts.'

She nodded again. She could picture it easily in her mind. The clouds whipping past the wide white face of the moon like torn rags. The winter storm surging across all those miles, hungry, furious, growing in strength until it came crashing into her shore like a hammer. Or, more aptly, a knife. For *this* storm had cut away the tough, razor-edged marram grass, dragging it out by its tenacious roots and flinging it far inland before starting in on the layers of dune below, stripping them away, flinging great sheets of sand into the sky, against her house, forcing the grit through every crack and into every cranny. Pity any living thing caught out in a storm like that, for it would surely have been the death of them!

And now, the morning after, she had more than enough to be doing, directing the men trying to get the water supply cleared – *the tea will taste brackish for weeks!* – keeping the servants at the cleaning, dealing with the thankfully minor injuries the weather-canny locals had sustained. She really hadn't time to be going out into the tail-end of the tempest and getting upset by damage she couldn't mend.

But Mr Trevelyan insisted.

So here they were, trudging through the last gusts of the storm, down to the poor battered shore to see ... what? She hoped it wasn't something stranded, dead or dying. Like a whale. Or a squid. They'd had one of those washed up the very first week she'd come to live in her new home – ghastly, yet pathetic at the same time. The stink of it had lingered long after the gulls and skuas finished tearing it to pieces.

I don't WANT to see something horrible, she was thinking, and so she wasn't looking ahead but focusing instead on where she was putting her feet and noticing how the blown sand that hissed round the bottom of her skirt sounded like spiteful snakes and wondering whether or not the leftover mutton would be enough for the cook to make a curry out of – Mr Trevelyan liked curry – when suddenly, they were there. At the shore.

But the shore had changed.

227

For a long moment she stood there staring, gaping the way a lady never should. It was as if she'd walked down to a different beach entirely. The green mound – the one the servants said belonged to the fairy folk – where was it?

'The Howe of the Trows – it's gone!'

And there were holes, there, where the mound had been. She stepped forward, struggling to keep hold of her hat in the gusts of sea wind, looked down and saw . . .

Houses! Little houses in the ground!

She had a sudden flashback to when she was a tiny girl, when she and her brothers had built a den in the woods, at her grandparents' place in the country, with bent branch walls and bracken thatch and wonky half-size beds. They'd stocked it with cracked teacups and mismatched plates and stolen biscuits from the kitchen and never, ever, quite had the nerve to sleep in it overnight . . .

'What do you think of that, then!' said her husband.

She turned to him in amazement, unable to think of anything coherent to say.

'Well? Don't wool-gather, my dear.' Mr Trevelyan sounded impatient.

'But what . . . who . . .?'

'Mr Trevelyan! Mrs Trevelyan! Isn't it *marvellous*?!'

A head appeared, followed by a dishevelled young man, rising up out of one of the holes in a shower of sand and excitement.

'Mr Lawrence?'

It was the new curate. Mr Trevelyan didn't rate his Sunday homilies very highly but she quite liked him. He reminded her of a large, ungainly, good-natured puppy.

228

The young man reached up to doff his hat, realised he wasn't wearing one, and sketched a bow instead.

'Your servant, madam.' He managed a decorous expression for less than a second before the boyish exhilaration burst out again. 'Isn't this the most amazing thing?!'

'It is, I'm sure – but *what* is it?'

His amiably ugly face was split by a wide grin. 'I think – no, I'm certain – that what we see before us is a miraculously preserved Neolithic village! Sir, Madam, I'd bet my best hat, which I appear to have lost, that this site – these houses – may very well date from the same time as the Ring of Brodgar, the stone circle at Stenness – perhaps Maeshowe itself! We have been given a glimpse – a window! – into that distant age, and not just the big gestures, the ritual sites – life wearing its Sunday best, so to speak – but ordinary people, living ordinary lives. A frozen moment, caught forever, hidden under the sand for thousands of years and now—' He did a little dance of excitement and came close to sliding back into the hole. 'Forgive my enthusiasm, but I believe that this is the closest to real time travel a human being can ever hope to come!'

Mr Trevelyan tutted scornfully, but Mrs Trevelyan warmed to the young man's exuberance.

'Then you feel this discovery is of importance, Mr Lawrence?' she asked him gently.

'Importance?! This is without doubt *the* most important archaeological discovery of the century! Of *any* century! It's huge – it's gigantic – it's . . .' He waved his hands, momentarily lost for words. He looked into Mrs Trevelyan's attentive face and went on, 'But even

229

more than that – it's the intimacy, the closeness, the . . . Madam, I feel as if the owners have only just stepped out a moment ago – I can *sense* them . . . I'm sure you understand me!'

'No, sir. My wife is not a fanciful person,' said Mr Trevelyan disapprovingly.

The curate blushed, but before she could say anything to soften the reproof, her husband caught sight of some of the farm boys, come to gawk at the holes.

'Hey!' he shouted, hurrying off to chivvy them with his stick. 'You there – get back to your work!'

Mr Lawrence turned to her. 'May I show you, madam? I have a ladder down into this first house that I'm sure you could manage . . .?' He was so eager, it would be impolite to disappoint him. And yet, just as she was about to step forward, she stopped with a shudder.

'I'm sorry – are you cold, Mrs Trevelyan?'

'No . . . thank you . . .' It wasn't the cold. But what *was* it? She shivered again. It was the strangest sensation, as if someone were standing behind her but when she turned, there was no one there. She smiled apologetically. 'It's nothing. Just a silly feeling. My nurse would have said it was someone walking over my grave.'

'A goose.' He smiled back at her. 'My nurse said it was a goose walking over my grave, but why a goose and not, say, a cow or a ferret, I never dared ask.' He really had the most engaging face.

Still she felt unsettled, anxious – afraid to go down the ladder and into the little house. She couldn't help looking over her shoulder again. *Mr Lawrence must be wondering what I'm dithering about.* She needed to give him some explanation, but she didn't understand herself . . .

230

And then she remembered something she thought he would understand.

'Mrs Trevelyan?' He sounded sincerely concerned.

So, as lightly as she could, she said, 'We are not long returned from a visit to the Continent in which we visited the archaeological site at Pompeii. I imagine my reluctance may arise from that.' She certainly wished never again to experience the sensations that had swept her at the sight of those poor, twisted bodies, the feeling of horror that blanketed the place as surely as the ash had done.

The curate's face cleared.

'Ah. I understand. Don't worry, madam. No skeletal remains have been found. There is nothing here you can't see.'

Her spine prickled again – she swung round, but of course there was no one there – and yet she was sure that this time she had *heard* something. A sound that was almost like a sigh . . . a sigh of relief . . .?

That is quite enough of that!

Mrs Trevelyan smiled firmly at the young man. 'Thank you – I would very much like to see what you have discovered,' she said as she took his hand to descend.

It was a fascinating tour, and Mr Lawrence promised to keep her apprised of all his discoveries as he continued the work of the wind in digging out the sand. Her husband returned to hand her back up the ladder and together they stood for a moment, looking down into the curate's upturned face.

'What happened here, Mr Lawrence?' asked Mr Trevelyan in a voice quieter than usual.

The young man shook his head. 'I expect we'll never know, sir. There is only so much we can learn about these people from what they left behind. Even modern science cannot answer every question.'

Again that feeling of someone standing near, someone she couldn't see. Was that a laugh she heard? Just on the edge of hearing?

Mrs Trevelyan smiled to herself and shook her head.

I am not a fanciful woman, she told the listening air, and picking up her skirts, she headed for home.

Epilogue

In fact, young Mr Lawrence was not completely accurate when he said that there were no bodies found at Skara Brae. Later excavations revealed two human skeletons, both women, buried in a stone cist under the floor of what is now known as House 7.

To date, archaeologists don't know why the women are there.

Note to Readers

So much of what we think we know about the time when the Stone Age was bleeding into the Bronze Age is based on bewildering artefacts and guesswork. What we *do* know, however, is that during this time, the climate worsened. There are many scientific, anthropological, archaeological theories about the effect climate change might have had on the civilisation of Orkney, and I have cherry-picked indiscriminately among them. This story is just that – a story. It is driven by the interactions of fictional characters in a setting that has sparked my own imagination for years. I have researched and visited museums and sites and taken photographs and talked and listened, but if you are looking in the result for a historical document, you will be disappointed.